Isabella and I hope you like the scary stories. Happy Holidays!

<u>Holiday</u>

Madness

13 Dark Tales for
Halloween, Christmas,
and All Occasions

Fred Wiehe

December 2010

BLACK BED
SHEET

Holiday Madness
A Black Bed Sheet/Diverse Media Book
October 2009

All stories were first read on KKUP radio in the San Francisco
Bay Area from 2004 through 2009.
Trick or Treat; It's the Puppet People was later published in *Sinister
Tales Magazine*, Halloween 2007.
Trick or Troll was later published at *ShadeWorks*, Halloween
2008.

Library of Congress Control Number: 2009910455

ISBN-10: 0-9842136-5-1
ISBN-13: 978-0-9842136-5-8

Holiday Madness

A Black Bed Sheet/Diverse Media Book
Antelope, CA

Also by Fred Wiehe:

Fiction:

Strange Days
The Burning
Night Songs
Starkville

Short Stories/novellas/anthologies:

Trick or Treat: It's the Puppet People
Trick or Troll

Nonfiction:

Creative Writing: Get Started Writing
Fiction

H/M

To my brothers and sisters:
Steve, Sandy, Sharon, Debbie, Craig, and
Kevin
Seven of us…now orphans all

In memory of my parents Fred (Fritz) and
Elizabeth (Betty)…now drinking beer and
dancing the jitterbug in heaven.

As always, thank you to my wife and children
for their never-ending support and love. I love
you Suzy, Jesse, and Jan.

I'd also like to thank my mother-in-law June and
my brother-in-law Steve for their support
throughout the years.

Of course, I have to thank Jim McMillen of
KKUP radio. Please read the Forward for
further understanding of how these 13 tales
wouldn't exist without him or the radio station.

Lastly, I hope all of my writing students—both
children and adults—at Communication
Academy, Sunnyvale-Cupertino Adult
Education, and Milpitas Adult Education enjoy
and learn from these 13 tales.

H/M

φ

H/M

"Halloween lurks
Within shadows in my head
Christmastime gremlins hide
Underneath my bed
Trolls crouch at my threshold
Wolf Men come to call
Ghosts haunt my thoughts
And walk my dusty halls
Uglies prowl the night
Hunting for helpless prey
Puppet People don't exist
At least that's what I hope
At least that's what I pray
Vampires step into sunlight
They burst into fire
It's at night that they hunt
It's my blood they desire
But none of these monsters compare
To the stresses and the sadness
Those crazy feelings I get
And strange voices that I hear
That I call holiday madness"

—The Collected Nightmares

H/M

H/M
TABLE OF CONTENTS:

H/M

Holiday Madness

Fred Wiehe

Forward

The tales you're about to read are a compilation of stories that I had written specially for radio station KKUP, 91.5 FM in the San Francisco Bay Area. Some years ago, my good friend and radio personality Jim McMillen somehow convinced me (or was it *conned* me) into writing a short story to read on his program *One from the Heart* at Christmas time. This to me seemed like a strange request since I'm basically a horror writer; Christmas and horror just didn't seem like a natural mix. Still, I agreed. But I knew (and warned Jim) that a Christmas story from a horror writer was going to be anything but traditional, fuzzy, or warm.

His response was, "Great!"

That first year *A Gremlin for Christmas* was born and so was what has become a new holiday tradition. Apparently, people loved the idea of dark, nontraditional Christmas stories.

We have now completed our fifth annual Christmas/Horror show at KKUP. The stories after that first year in succession are *Holiday Madness*; *The Three Wolf Men*; *Run, Run Rudy: A Zombie's Not Too Far Behind*; and *Santa's War*. For Christmas 2009, I'll be reading *Christmas-Time Gremlins* (a sequel to *A Gremlin for Christmas*), which is also included in this anthology.

Putting me to work once a year and having a successful, annual Christmas show, however, wasn't enough for Jim. Soon he came to me with the more logical idea of having an annual Halloween show. This of course seemed like a more natural fit for a horror writer. But of course, now he had me writing two stories a year for his show. Let me tell you folks there's nothing like working for free.

But I couldn't say no, so three successful Halloween programs later we have *Trick or Treat: It's the Puppet People*; *Trick or Troll*; and *The Uglies*. By the way, those first two stories were later published in Halloween editions of *Sinister Tales Magazine* and *ShadeWorks* respectively, as well as in this anthology. For Halloween 2009, I've given him two for the price of one: the short story, *Ghosts, Inc.*, and the poem, *The Halloween Box*. Of course, these two are also included in this anthology.

In between the annual holiday shows, Jim also had me appear on two Talk Marathons for KKUP and had me on his show a couple of times during the summer, usually when another guest bailed at the last second. Two more stories were born because of those guest spots but without holiday themes: *Raven Mocker* and *Bad Moon*. These two stories round out this collection.

I have to say that it's been my privilege to be a part of KKUP, 91.5FM in Cupertino, California and Jim's show—*One from the Heart*. The radio station is a public, nonprofit station, and all of its on-air personalities and staff are volunteers. It survives solely on donations by its listeners. It's also been an honor to entertain those listeners and to help raise money for this worthy station.

I'd also like to thank Jim McMillen for forcing me to write these stories; without him this anthology wouldn't exist. I've had a great time reading them on air and talking with listeners from around the San Francisco Bay Area. I hope to continue this tradition for many years to come too.

But now it's come time to share these nontraditional Christmas stories and Halloween stories, as well as the two other stories for all occasions with a much wider audience; that's the purpose of compiling these 13 (my favorite number) tales into book form.

It's my hope that readers—Tweens, Teens, Young Adults, and Adults alike—from all over and from all walks of life enjoy these supernatural tales as much as the listeners of KKUP radio in the Bay Area enjoyed hearing them.

Happy Halloween!
Merry Christmas!

Be scared!

Fred Wiehe

October 2009

Fred Wiehe

Holiday
Madness

The alien voices start right after Thanksgiving. At first, they are just whisperings in my head, like a hundred hissing snakes slithering in and out of my mind—incomprehensible, garbled, and perplexing. They make no sense to me. I can't decipher one from another. I suppose it could even be one voice that endlessly echoes through my mind, as if not for this constant chatter my head would be an empty and cavernous void. But I suspect they are many voices, bombarding me like a demonic blitzkrieg.

Why I think the voices are the work of the devil and not God, I can't tell you. I can't understand what they're saying. I can't translate their message. I have no idea for certain if the voices communicate good or evil. But a cold, greasy sensation deep in my soul, like an oil spill on the ocean, warns me of the possibility for wickedness. A volcanic rumbling in my once dormant gut cautions me against listening.

Still, I find it next to impossible to turn a deaf ear. The voices are relentless, feeding on my brain

1

as a pack of ravenous wolves feed on dead prey, ripping and rending my will to shreds. I try to pay no heed to them and go about my daily chores as if all's right with the world. Christmas, after all, is fast approaching; this is a time for joy and hope, a time for giving and family. So, I work at my job, kiss my wife, play with the kids, tend the stock, and make my Christmas lists as usual. But I do so without much enthusiasm, and always with the whispers as constant and unwelcome companions.

Only a week before Christmas and the voices grow louder, clearer, more distinct. Rather than a jumble of whisperings that sound like so much white noise, I can now tell one voice from the other and even somewhat decipher what they're trying to tell me. I can't understand every word but a few come through loud and clear: IMPOSTERS...DANGER...DEAD.

Now, rather than trying to ignore the voices, I listen to them carefully for better understanding. Clearly, they're attempting to warn me, to save me from some sort of impending threat. I no longer believe they're demonic in nature but instead voices of salvation, wishing nothing more than to deliver me from harm's way. The harder I concentrate the more I'm rewarded with clarity of mind, until finally the voices meld into one clear message:

"You are in danger. Don't trust the imposters. They want you dead."

The now intelligible message raises more questions than it answers, disturbing questions with no ready answers:

Imposters? What imposters? Who are these people that want me dead? Why do they want me

2

dead?

Paranoia now clings to me like a funeral shroud. Fear and suspicion feed on my wits until only bare bones remain. I jump at every sound and from the corner of my eye I see inexplicable movement in every dark corner and every shadow. I bite my fingernails to nubs as worry plagues my soul. I eye everyone with wariness and mistrust. Those closest to me are of most concern—my wife, my children. I no longer look upon them with loving eyes but rather with misgivings and doubts. Soon, however, this simple apprehension gives way to anxiety, which in turn gives way to panic, and then eventually becomes pure terror.

All the while, the message rings through my head like an SOS:

"You are in danger. Don't trust the imposters. They want you dead."

I can no longer stand the sight of my family. They are indeed the imposters the voice warns me about; they must be, for there's no one else here. They seem like strangers to me, almost alien in nature, as if no longer human. How could they have fooled me for so long? Why hadn't I seen what they'd become? Are they witches, using some kind of glamour? Was I under a spell that is now broken? No matter. I now see them for what they truly are— monsters who want me dead.

For protection, I distance myself from everyone and everything, a self-imposed hermit, if not physically at least emotionally. I no longer eat the food my wife prepares for fear of poisoning. Unfortunately, however, I grow more emaciated and weak by the day. But it can't be helped. I no longer

3

play with the children for fear they will somehow harm me with their scissors or jump ropes or sling shots. I even ignore all conversation, their voices sounding to me like demonic talons scraping across the prison walls in perdition. Even the children's laughter and songs bear the screeching tones of tortured souls. I dare not even make eye contact for fear that one look from them might strike me down as surely as Medusa's stare could turn me to stone. Even the animals have begun to exhibit cold, predatory looks about them, as if eating me is the sole purpose of their meager existence.

Danger surrounds me. Terror holds me hostage.

It's Christmas Eve. I lie in my bed, exhausted—having not slept for more than a week—but still awake. I dare not close my eyes, even for a second. I listen to the sleeping snores of the thing that used to be my wife lying next to me and wonder if she's faking sleep in the hope that I'll let down my guard and fall asleep myself. Yes, that's it, I'm sure. Once I'm asleep she'll plunge a knife deep into my chest or hold a pillow over my face. She wants me dead. They all do.

Rather than take a chance on falling asleep, I sneak out of bed and dress in work clothes and boots. Fatigue, starvation, and fright have rattled me senseless. I prowl the dark house like a brainless zombie. I must do something to save myself before inaction does the job for them. Soon I'll either die of hunger or collapse in a weakened state. Then I'll be at their mercy. Maybe even the stress and lack of sleep could cause a heart attack or stroke. I must do something. I need a plan.

But what?

My mind is like a cluttered attic full of cobwebs. I can't think. Nothing will come to me. Only the voice echoes its warning through me:

"You are in danger. Don't trust the imposters. They want you dead."

I'm going to go crazy. I'm sure of it. I must do something.

I tiptoe back into the bedroom. The thing pretending to be my wife still fakes sleep.

I must do something.

That's when I see it. An axe leans against the fireplace, next to the small stockpile of wood. At the sight of it, the message in my head changes:

"Kill them first! Before they kill you!"

I grin at the sudden insight. Cobwebs in my brain are abruptly knocked away, as if someone with a broom had just whisked through my head. Thoughts are clearer than they've been for weeks. Why hadn't I thought of it before? It's such a simple yet effective plan:

"Kill them first! Before they kill you!"

I creep to the fireplace. Floorboards squeak underfoot but the thing pretending to be my wife doesn't stir. I grab the axe handle and heft the heavy tool into the air. I bring it up and rest it on my shoulder as I approach the bed.

"Kill them first! Before they kill you!"

I nod as if in agreement. With both hands on the handle now, I raise the axe overhead. Like a rattle snake, I'm poised for a deadly strike. But she—it—awakens just before the first blow, as if I had somehow actually rattled a warning. She rolls over, peers up at me through the darkness, and terror sweeps across her face. In that moment, I'm no

5

longer sure of my convictions. I no longer see an alien or a monster. For the first time in weeks, I again see my wife. Her eyes plead with me to stop. She screams.

But I can't stop.

"Kill them first! Before they kill you!"

The axe plummets down as if possessed by an evil spirit. Heavy metal clunks loudly against skull. Blood splatters me, raining up onto my face and chest as if gravity didn't exist. I raise the axe again. Globs of blood and matted hair cling to the blade. The axe plummets. A torrential up-pour of red rain splatters me again. Bone fragments follow, pelting me like macabre shrapnel. But I don't stop. Again and again the axe falls, until only a mangled and bloody mass of flesh and bone fragments remain where her head had once been.

I'm sickened but not finished. The voice in my head still commands me:

"Kill them first! Before they kill you!"

I turn away when I'm sure she can no longer harm me. I pad to the large room where the aliens pretending to be my children sleep. As I push it open, the door creaks like a graveyard's rusted gate. No one wakes. They had slept through the screams and the sickening sound of the chopping axe, so why would a creaking door rouse them. I approach the first bed and hoist the axe overhead. The axe drops like the blade of a guillotine, but the thing on the bed rolls at the last second and it misses its mark. I quickly chop at the imposter again, but this time the blade crashes into the headboard and splinters it in two.

As if this was a call to arms, the imposters all

startle awake, screams on their lips. They scatter like scared rabbits at the sight of me and my axe. Little had they realized; I was on to their charade and their murderous plans. But now they know, and they run in panic for their lives.

I quickly give chase, brandishing my weapon as if on a holy war. I swing wildly at the scrambling imposters. I'm manic in my pursuit. My axe smashes bric-a-brac and tears into furniture and walls. Destruction is left in my wake by my blind rage. But all of the little aliens somehow manage to get out of the house unscathed, as if protected from my axe by black magic.

I stare from inside the open door. None of them are in sight, but I see their small footprints in the snow. Some head toward the forest. I needn't worry about them. They will surely freeze to death by morning. Most of the footprints lead to the barn. They think they're the smart ones. It's warm in there and there are places to hide—dark corners, mounds of hay. But I'll find them.

Undaunted, I give pursuit out into the frigid winter air. A stiff north wind greets me, and an icy downpour stings my face, like the thousand needles of an acupuncturist gone mad. Plumes of panted, frozen breath escape from my mouth, looking like wisps of tiny ghosts taking flight into the night. Hard surface snow crunches underfoot as I march across the yard. But I'm not the least bit cold. A maddening fire burns deep within the pit of my stomach, stoked by a combination of rage and the need to survive. Blood boils in my veins. I must find them all.

"Kill them first! Before they kill you!"

7

I must kill them all.

I kick in the barn door with the heel of my heavy boot. It smashes inward and bounces off the inside wall. I hear scuffling and muffled cries as I enter, but I see no movement, no sign of life except for the stock. The animals sense danger. They snort and stomp agitated hooves. A few kick their stable walls, splintering wood in their attempt to escape. But there will be no escape.

"Come out, come out, wherever you are," I call to the imposters that have taken over the lives of my children.

They don't come out. They're smarter than that, devious in their thinking. I'm sure they are busy concocting a murderous plan. I must act quickly, before they're able to put their plan into action.

Frustration and fury motivate me to hatch my own plan first. I'll get them to come out, one way or another. With the frenzy of a madman, I start hacking away at the stabled wildlife. The barn echoes with ululate cries and protracted bleats of frightened animals that instinctually realize they're all about to be put to slaughter. The butcher's axe has already sliced up three, and the sickening stench of the carnage has whipped the others into a frenzied panic.

I'm chopping the head off a fourth, showering in its blood, when the things that used to be my children rush me. They come out of nowhere, from every direction, pouncing on me en masse. The axe flies from my grasp as I go down hard on my back. Hands scratch at my face, poke at my eyes, and pull at the corners of my mouth. I try to fend them off, but there are too many of them. I'm defenseless.

They know it and laugh wickedly at my plight. The hideous, evil laughter renews my courage and strength. With a deep, guttural growl and a last-ditch effort, I push up and fling them away. They shoot into the air like exploding fireworks and tumble onto the floor.

I sit up in bed, panting as if I'd just run a marathon.

In bed? How did I get in bed?

I look around, disoriented and confused. Laughter fills my head.

"Papa, get up," my wife says, framed in the bedroom doorway.

Her face is no longer a mangled piece of flesh and bone. There's no blood. She looks normal.

"You've got a big night ahead of you," she says, "but you must eat first."

I'm dazed, still half asleep, not comprehending what she's telling me. I still can't get over that she's alive.

"Kris," she says, "are you all right?"

The elves are disentangling themselves on the floor, giggling all the while. Obviously, they thought my throwing them was all in fun because they had tried to wake me so forcefully.

"Yeah, come on, Santa," one elf says as he stands and brushes himself off, "the reindeer are hitched to the sleigh and ready to go."

I can hear the snorting and hoof stomping of the reindeer outside my window.

"All of you out," Mrs. Claus scolds the elves. "Let Santa wake up."

The elves scamper out the door, giggling and

playfully wrestling as they go.

I swing my legs over the side of the bed and place my feet on the cold floor. My hand swipes across my face to wipe the sleep away.

"Kris?" Mrs. Claus prompts.

"Yes, Mamma, I'm fine," I assure her. "I'll be right there."

She smiles weakly and leaves me alone.

I sit on the edge of the bed and struggle to get my bearings. The nightmare still haunts me, but I attribute it to the stress of the season. Each year is more hectic than the last, a big push to finish on time. It's taken its toll on my system. I haven't slept well for weeks, and I've lost weight. I know I don't look like the jolly old elf of story and song. But after tonight, I'll be able to rest, take some time off before starting on next year. The nightmares will end. I'm sure of it.

I stand on the legs of a landlubber at sea. Somehow I catch my balance before it's too late. From the corner of my eye, as I dress in my red suit and black boots, I catch a glimpse of the axe. It leans against the fireplace by the small stockpile of wood, its usual place.

It was just a nightmare, I tell myself, *nothing more than a terrible nightmare.*

But my gaze lingers on the axe, as if the mere sight of it holds my mind hostage.

And like a hundred hissing snakes, cold, whispering voices slither in and out of my head, bombarding me like a demonic blitzkrieg.

10

Trick or Treat: It's the Puppet People

I remember Halloween 1979. Maybe it's the last thing I truly remember. It's been thirty years, but in some ways it feels as if it happened yesterday. In other ways it feels like a lifetime ago. It doesn't really matter; the horror of that night will never leave me. No matter how much time passes:

Storm clouds blanketed the night sky, holding the stars and moon hostage. The smell of rain and ozone mixed together and filled the cold, night air. Far away, thunder rumbled like a waking dragon, its hot, fiery breath flashing in the distant horizon. Periodically, fat dragon tears splattered us and the pavement.

We knew we better hurry. The storm threatened and we were already chilled to the bone. But we wanted to collect as much candy as possible before being driven indoors for the night. Mom and Dad made us promise to be home before the rain came, and the thunder and lightning hadn't started at all before we left. Otherwise, they never would have let us go trick or treating.

I was only eight. My brother Charlie was twelve. We dressed as hobos in old clothes, and we rubbed burnt cork on our faces to make us look as though we needed shaves. Both of us had on old hats too. Our bags were old pillowcases that looked like a bundle of our earthly possessions when filled with candy to complete the makeshift costumes.

We hadn't had much time to put the costumes together because just days ago we had moved to Cincinnati, thousands of miles away from the only home we had ever known, thousands of miles away from all of our friends back in California. It might as well been China. We'd never see our friends again. We both knew that.

I think that's the only reason Mom and Dad let us go out; they felt sorry for us. They hadn't even finished unpacking yet. But the first room they did finish was the upstairs bedroom Charlie and I shared. They had even hung my cowboy scene on the wall next to my bed—a four-piece set of cardboard, cartoon cutouts that consisted of a singing cowboy strumming a guitar, a dog howling along to the music, a campfire, and a covered wagon.

When we first started out, trick or treating together had helped us feel a bit better. But now those fat dragon tears turned to a steady cry. And as we trudged toward our new home, our moods darkened again. Yes, our pillowcases were laden with sweet handouts, but we were wet, cold, and probably in trouble for not getting back sooner.

12

As we passed a large brick house, Charlie brightened and said, "This house is still lit up, Petey. Let's make one more stop."

I shivered, soaked to the bone now, water dripping from the brim of my old hat, my pillowcase heavy in my grasp. "I don't know, Charlie. I think we best get home. Mom and Dad are gonna be mad."

Lightning flashed and thunder rumbled, urging us home.

Charlie looked skyward. "Ah, it's just a drizzle. The real storm is still far away."

I looked doubtful.

Lightning flashed on the horizon. Thunder followed quickly on its heels.

"See," Charlie said. "The lightning's still off in the distance and the thunder took a full ten seconds or more after it flashed."

"I've got enough candy," I said pleadingly. "I'm wet and cold."

Charlie punched my shoulder. "Killjoy," he said.

But we started walking again rather than trick or treating more. And he had pulled his punch; it hadn't really hurt.

We were almost home when Charlie said, "Did you know our new house is haunted?"

"You're lying," I said quickly. "You're just trying to scare me, is all."

Charlie shrugged. "Trying to warn you, is all. I care about you. You're my little bro."

"Yeah, right," I said.

Charlie shrugged again. "Be that way," he said.

A bolt of lightning ripped open the sky overhead. What sounded like a sonic boom

13

immediately followed.

We both froze and looked skyward.

"Holy…" Charlie started to say but never got the chance to finish.

Rain poured down on us as if the lightning really had punctured a hole in the sky. We took off running, pretending Halloween phantoms chased us to make us go faster, feet slapping through the puddles quickly forming on the sidewalk.

In two short blocks we were safe inside our new house. Dressed and with car keys in hand, Dad was heading for the door as we burst through it. Mom was right behind him.

"I was just getting ready to go out and look for you two," Dad said.

Mom said, "Look at you two. You're both soaked."

Dad shook his head but didn't seem to have the heart to scold us. "Get upstairs and get dry. Both of you get straight into your pajamas and then into bed."

We both grinned at him and took off up the stairs.

He yelled after us, "Only one piece of candy each before bed too. No more."

Mom added, "Make sure you brush your teeth after."

Dry and in my pajamas, I climbed into bed. But I knew sleep wouldn't come fast. It wasn't just the flashes of light and claps of thunder outside our window or the rain pounding against the glass as if desperately wanting in. I couldn't get what Charlie had told me—just before the rain bombarded us—out of my head. But I also wasn't sure I wanted to ask either. Maybe it would be better not to know.

In the end, I couldn't help myself.

When Charlie came out of the bathroom, dry and in his pajamas, I asked, "What did you mean?"

Charlie gave me a quizzical expression. "What did I mean about what?"

"You know," I stammered, "about the house being haunted."

Behind Charlie, lightning flashed at the window. He grinned demonically as thunder rumbled like an angry ogre.

"Oh, that," Charlie said.

I tried not to show I was scared, but shivers attacked my body, giving me away.

Charlie came over and sat on my bed. We both faced the wall and the closet next to my bed.

"Haven't you noticed the face on the closet door and the eyes all over the walls?" he asked.

I shook my head and gulped down what felt like a rock in my throat.

"Look," he said, pointing at the door and the walls.

I did. The door was wooden. The walls were paneled wood. I shook my head again.

"Look closer," he said. "See the face in the wood grain of the door. See the dark eyes in the paneling of the walls?"

Sure enough, they were there. Why hadn't I noticed before? The grain on the door looked like a long face, with a bushy beard. The face had big, dark eyes, with long lashes. Not only that, thousands of pairs of beady eyes marked the surrounding walls—dark, penetrating gazes locked onto us.

"Th-that's not a face … and th-those aren't e-e-

15

e-eyes," I stammered.

"Sure," Charlie said, "you think it's just the grain and knotholes in the wood. But at night, in the dark, they come alive. The Puppet People use them to watch us from their dimension—the fourth dimension."

I gulped, the rock still lodged in my throat. "The P-P-Puppet People?" I stammered. "Who are they?"

Charlie again grinned demonically. "They're beings from the fourth dimension. They watch us at night. If you stare at the face long enough in the dark, you'll see the eyes blink. Stare at the eyes in the wall and you'll see the dark pupils following your movements. They're called the Puppet People."

"Charlie…what are they? What do they want?"

"They want us," Charlie answered in a hush, secretive. "But they can't get us. They can only watch us." He paused, gulping down a stone too. "Excepting on Halloween, that is."

My heart slammed against my chest. "Halloween?"

Charlie nodded. They're called the Puppet People because they can inhabit inanimate objects."

"What-what are those? Inamminit opjits?"

Charlie laughed nervously. "No…no. Inanimate objects, you little dweeb. That means things that aren't alive and can't move, like your cowboy on the wall."

I stared at my cowboy with new wonder. I gasped as lightning flashed through the window and across the cowboy's face. When thunder boomed seconds later, the cowboy shook on its nail, as if already coming to life.

Undaunted, Charlie continued, "On Halloween they can escape their dimension and bring things to life that aren't alive. They can turn your cowboy into their evil puppet. Go ahead, tonight stare at your cowboy in the dark, really concentrate, and you'll see him come alive. That's them crossing over from their dimension into ours, using the cowboy to do their evil bidding."

I shook my head so hard it hurt. "You're lying, Charlie. There's no such thing."

"I'm not lying," Charlie insisted. "I'm trying to warn you. On Halloween the Puppet People can do more than just watch us, I swear. Halloween is when they come for us. They want to steal our souls, make us one of them, take us back to their dimension."

"Charlie, stop!" I yelled, covering my ears with both hands. I started crying, tears as big and fat as the dragon's earlier, except these weren't cold but rather hot with fear.

Lightning flashed. Thunder boomed.

Charlie forced my hands down. He yelled over the ongoing storm outside our window. "You're only hope is to watch for them. Stare at the face. You'll see the eyes start blinking. Stare at the eyes in the walls. You'll see them watching you. Then stare at the cowboy. When you see him start moving then you'll know they're coming. Hide under your covers. It's your only hope. Maybe they won't see you. Maybe they won't find you. But don't make a sound. Pretend you're sleeping. They can only take you if you're awake. They can only take you if they can see and taste your fear."

I screamed.

Charlie laughed.

Lightning flashed. Thunder boomed.

The door to our room opened. Dad stuck his head inside. "What's going on?" he yelled. He looked at me, saw my tears and the fear etched across my face. "Charlie, stop scaring your brother. I know it's Halloween but really, Charlie, do you have to torture him?"

Charlie said nothing.

"Petey," Dad continued, voice softening, "Charlie's just messing with you. You know that, right?"

I choked back my tears and nodded.

"Good," Dad said. "There's nothing here that can harm you. No matter what Charlie says, right, Charlie?"

Charlie said nothing.

"Right, Charlie?" Dad repeated more sternly.

"Uh…yeah, right," Charlie said. "Right, Dad."

Dad gave Charlie a firm look. "Now, both of you get in bed."

Charlie scrambled off of my bed and into the bed against the far wall, under the window. I lay down and scrunched under the covers.

"Lights out," Dad said, switching off the overhead light and plunging us into darkness, except for the soft glow from the tiny, Darth Vader night light plugged into the wall socket and the occasional flash of lightning from outside. "No messing around, you two. Get to sleep." He started closing our door. Before it was completely closed, he said, "Goodnight, I love you both."

I lay there, covers pulled to my chin, my back to Charlie. I said nothing and neither did my brother. I listened to the storm raging outside. As my eyes

18

slowly adjusted to the dark, I stared at the closet door, at that long face with the bushy beard and dark eyes ingrained into the wood. I knew I should go to sleep, like Dad said, but I couldn't close my eyes for fear I'd miss the signs of the Puppet People's attack. If they came for me then I wanted to know it.

The long eyelashes blinked.

I gasped, almost screamed out, but choked it down. Charlie said to not let them know I was awake, to pretend to be asleep. But my eyes widened rather than closed. I couldn't tear my gaze away from that horrid face.

The long lashes blinked faster and faster. The bushy beard whipped about in a stiff wind I couldn't feel. Lightning flashed across it. Thunder shook the house.

Not able to stand the sight anymore, I ripped my gaze away. But I couldn't pretend it didn't happen; it was the first warning sign that they were coming for us. I searched the walls, staring at the sets of eyes littering it. They didn't move. They seemed as lifeless and as empty as that of a corpse. But that gave me little comfort, so I concentrated harder, staring at the eyes through the darkness. Then I saw it, the second sign.

All of the beady eyes came alive at once, blinking, searching the room for signs of life that they could take back with them, souls to steal.

I cried out. I couldn't help myself. Immediately, I realized my mistake. Immediately, all of the eyes focused on me. I cursed the thunder for its sudden silence. Why couldn't it have covered my cry? The Puppet People now knew I was there. They would be coming for me.

I looked to my cowboy scene. Charlie had said that when I saw the cowboy move I would know they were coming. I concentrated, unblinking, staring at the scene on my wall. A cold sweat trickled down my back. The foul taste of fear soured my mouth and dried up my spit. I almost choked on it as I waited.

I didn't have to wait long. The cowboy slowly began to strum soundlessly on his guitar as he sang a wordless, tuneless song. Next to him, the hound dog raised its head and howled silently to the heavens. The flames of the campfire flickered and danced, crackling wood nonexistent. The wheels of the covered wagon spun wildly but noiselessly, as if racing across the prairie of a silent movie.

They were coming. The Puppet People were coming for my soul.

With that single thought, sparkling specters emerged from where walls met ceiling. They quietly swirled about the room overhead, like vultures I'd seen on cowboy movies that circled the desert for something dead to feed on. But I had the feeling these ghostly vultures searched for live prey, souls to steal.

I clamped my eyes shut and threw the covers up and over my head, hiding in a frightened heap under them, praying it wasn't too late to fool the horrid creatures. But fear clutched me in a tight grip, shaking me, rattling me, throttling me. I couldn't stop it, even though I knew the movement would give me away. My teeth chattered uncontrollably, loudly, further giving me away. The thunder had abandoned me completely. The night was now silent except for my chattering teeth and heavy, frightened breath. I was doomed. I knew it in my heart. But still, I prayed the covers would protect me the same as a force field on *Star Trek*.

But it didn't.

Hundreds of hands touched me, pawed at me through the covers, probing their way to me.

A scream shattered the surrounding silence. I thought it was me but then realized I hadn't made a sound except for my chattering teeth and the weak whimpers of a scared puppy. Seconds later, another scream ricocheted about the room—piercing and high-pitched.

It was Charlie.

The hands left me. I no longer felt them probing at the covers. Had I fooled them or had they been attracted to my brother's wails?

Take him, not me, I prayed. *Take him, not me.*

Even as I wished it, guilt stabbed me in the heart. But I couldn't help myself. I couldn't stop.

Take him, not me. Take him, not me. Take him, not me.

Charlie screamed again. Long and agonizing, as if the Puppet People torturously ripped his soul from inside him.

I didn't call for help. I didn't try to help him myself. Instead, I kept my eyes clamped shut and hid under the covers, thumb stuck in my mouth like a little baby.

Take him, not me… take him, not me… take him, not me… take him, not me…

The next morning I woke, covers still pulled up over my head, thumb still stuck into my mouth. The room was mercifully quiet—no storm, no screaming. I took my thumb out of my mouth, embarrassed even though no one could see me. I threw the covers off and was greeted by sunshine streaming in through the window. Charlie wasn't in bed.

He must be up, I told myself.

I was sure that it had all just been a nightmare. There was no such thing as the Puppet People. It all seemed silly in the light of day. Charlie had been messing with me, and I had had a nightmare, is all.

I hopped out of bed. I looked at the closet door and sighed in relief. The face was nothing more than the wood grain. The eyes on the walls again just looked like knotholes. But when I looked at the cowboy, my own breath choked me, like a noose around my neck.

Charlie's face replaced the cartoon face of the cowboy, his mouth open wide not in song but in an agonizing, silent scream, his eyes wide with terror. My prayers had been answered. They took him, not me.

I peed in my pajamas and screamed.

It's the last thing I truly remember. The last thing I remember. The last thing I remember...truly, truly remember...the last thing...the last thing I remember...

♦♦♦

On Halloween, thirty years later, Charlie stepped into Petey's private room. The light from the hallway stabbed at the darkness through the open doorway. He closed the door, killing the light, and stumbled through the dark to the side of the hospital bed. He sat in the chair next to the bed and waited for his eyesight to adjust. Grief squeezed his heart in a devilish grip. Guilt clung to his soul like a disposed ghost. The only reason he'd come back to town was to bury his Dad; Mom had passed more than five years earlier. He hadn't come to visit Petey since. But now it fell to Charlie to take care of his little brother. Petey had no one else left in the world.

It's the way it should be, Charlie thought. *After all, it was his fault that Petey lay in a coma these past thirty years, a vegetable.*

Lightning flashed outside the window and thunder rumbled in the distance like a waking dragon.

Charlie's eyes adjusted to the dark. He could now make out the sleeping man-child that was his brother. He thought of Petey that way. In Charlie's heart and mind his brother would be forever eight years old. The only reality of Petey as a man lay silently in bed.

Mercifully, blankets covered most of Petey's skeletal form. His brother breathed on his own, but received nourishment through a tube in his stomach and an IV in his arm. The last time Charlie saw Petey, he looked close to death—emaciated and gaunt, hair brittle, skin grey as a corpse. Charlie shivered at the thought of how his little brother must look now, five years later. That's why he dared not turn on the light. He didn't think he could stand the sight. It would only increase the guilt and pain that already fed on his soul like vultures ripping at a dead carcass.

The distant, waking dragon breathed fire, flashing light against the window pane and across the darkened room. The thing rumbled after, as if hungry.

23

Charlie paid the oncoming storm no mind. He was lost in guilt. He'd never forgiven himself, and probably never would, for telling the story of the Puppet People to his little brother that Halloween. He had literally scared his brother into a catatonic state. The next morning, they had found Petey collapsed on the floor next to his bed, pajamas soaked with urine, mumbling incoherently. They had tried wakening him but couldn't. Charlie was convinced even then, and still, that his brother would never again open his eyes. Sometimes Charlie even thought that maybe the Puppet People really did exist and that they had come that night and had stolen Petey's soul. Sometimes he imagined that this was nothing more than an empty shell lying in bed next to him and that Petey now lived in the fourth dimension.

But that was stupid. He knew that. The Puppet People didn't exist. He had made them up to scare his little brother on Halloween.

He'd done a fine job of that, hadn't he?

Tears welled in his eyes, further hindering his eyesight. He wiped them away.

Lightning flashed across the room.

That's when he saw it. The cowboy scene from their youth hung on the wall nearest Petey's bed. Dad must've hung it there, hoping the familiarity of it would have a positive affect on Petey.

Thunder rumbled—closer.

A new pang of guilt stabbed at Charlie's heart; he had never admitted the Puppet People story to either Dad or Mom. They had had no idea that the cowboy scene was a part of Petey's horrible ordeal that sent him spiraling into his catatonic state. They

24

had had no idea that Charlie's scary story was responsible for Petey's fate.

Charlie had been afraid to tell them at first, afraid they'd hate him. And as time passed, it just seemed easier to keep the secret than admit to it, no matter how heavy it weighed on him.

Rain beat against the window as if wanting to get inside at him. Charlie ignored it. He stared through the darkness at the cowboy, cursing the cartoon cutout, cursing himself.

The cowboy slowly began to strum soundlessly on his guitar as he sang a wordless, tuneless song.

Charlie choked on his own breath at the sight. But his gaze remained locked onto the cowboy's insidious cartoon face.

His mind screamed, *It's Halloween! The Puppet People are coming!*

Lightning flashed. Thunder boomed.

The cowboy's cartoon face blurred in Charlie's vision as tears welled in his eyes. He wiped the tears away, but no matter how hard he stared, he could no longer make out the cowboy's features.

The Puppet People are coming! Halloween! The Puppet People are coming!

The cowboy's face slowly came back into focus. But it wasn't the same. Somehow, it had changed. Transformed.

Charlie stared hard at it in disbelief. He peed in his pants and whispered, "Petey?"

Fred Wiehe

A Gremlin for Christmas

A gremlin came
On Christmas day
It came as a stowaway
On Santa's sleigh

It had dagger-like teeth
And massive pointy claws
Even though it stood
Barely four feet tall

Knotted, tangled hair
Sprouted from head to toe
Beady, red eyes
Darted to and fro

It looked like the spawn
Of demon seed
It had a deep-seated hunger
A ravenous need to feed

On human flesh
It wished to sink its teeth
Ripping and rending
A Christmas feast

Fred Wiehe

To this end
It hid in Santa's bag
To find a home, a family to eat
On Christmas day

Santa didn't know
The little beast had tagged along
A present not from him
For an unsuspecting child, dad, and mom

Santa climbed from the sleigh
Presents slung over his back
And slid down the chimney
With the demon, the gremlin stowaway
Hidden in his sack

While the jolly, old elf
Put all the gifts underneath the tree
The beastie climbed out of the sack
Finally free

It crept to the shadows
In a far off corner
There, it lurked, it waited, bided its time
While Santa finished
With the family's Christmas order

Mr. Claus took
One last look around the room
He suddenly had an unexplained chill
An impending feeling of doom

Holiday Madness

He stroked his white whiskers
And eyed the shadows
But he was by nature good and saintly
An unsuspecting fellow

So with a shrug of his shoulders
And a tinkling of a Christmas bell
He was back up the chimney
Unknowingly leaving behind
The terrible thing from Hell

The gremlin chuckled with evil glee
As it watched Santa go
Pleased to no end with itself
As it stepped out from its hiding place
Deep within the shadows

It crept to the staircase
And climbed them slow and steady
Its massive, pointy claws
And its sharp, deadly teeth
Ever at the ready

It snuck down the gloomy hall
And searched for its feast
Following its nose
Sniffing the scent of human blood, human flesh
The sinful little beast

It stopped cold at the doorway
Of an unsuspecting boy
The soft glow of a nightlight
Exposed a floor cluttered with toys

29

Fred Wiehe

It looked as though
A terrible tornado had touched down and struck
In this case the tornado was the little boy
The little boy named Chuck

Chuck lay beneath the covers
All snuggly and warm
He slept the sleep of youthfulness
(Deep and unsuspecting)
And he dreamt the dreams of innocence
(Unaware of danger impending)
Not at all forewarned

The gremlin licked his lips with delight
At the prospect of eating the boy
It crept into the room with stealth, with grace
Until it accidentally stepped on a toy

The toy made a loud squeak
A terrible noise
That echoed through the room
And awakened the sleeping boy

Chuck scanned his tiny bedroom
After jerking awake
Then let out a horrified squeal
As if he'd just seen a snake

But it wasn't a snake, a spider
Or even a slimy snail
It was much more terrible than that
What he saw was the gremlin
And the sight of it turned the boy pale

Holiday Madness

The gremlin let out a piercing shriek
And bared razor-sharp teeth
It flew at the boy
Eager to start the feast

Its claws swiped through the air
Aiming at Chuck's face
But luckily missed
And that's what started the race

Chuck bounded out of bed
And scrambled underneath
From there he shot across the room and out the door
With the quickest of feet

He ran down the hallway
With the gremlin right behind
Searching for help
It was his mom and dad he had to find

But the gremlin tripped him up
Just as he passed the top of the stairs
Together they tumbled down them
An unsightly pair

They hit the bottom hard
With a mighty thump
The boy lay very still and quiet
In a semiconscious lump

Fred Wiehe

But the gremlin rolled free
And bounded to its hairy feet
It came at the dazed and woozy boy
Ready to eat

It licked its lips with evil glee
And it drooled with anticipation
Was there no one to help this boy?
Was there no one to offer salvation?

The gremlin raised its pointed claws
Ready to rip and rend
But before the wicked thing could strike
A shovel smacked it upside the head

The sound of metal on bone
Echoed throughout the house
The shovel cracked the thing's skull wide open
Bone fragments, tissue, and blood
Spraying all about

The gremlin swayed unsteady
On big, hairy feet
Then it crashed to the floor
In a big, hairy heap

Its beady red eyes
Rolled back inside its head
There was no doubt about it
Very much, the gremlin was dead

Holiday Madness
Santa dropped his shovel
And took the boy gently in his arms
He hugged Chuck with all his might
Glad to have kept him from harm

Chucks arms went around Santa's neck
And hugged the jolly, old elf right back
He whispered in Santa's ear
"Thank you for saving me, Santa
Thank you for coming back"

Santa carried Chuck to a chair
And sat down with the boy on his lap
Santa said, "I'm sorry Chuck
I feel like a giant sap
I brought that gremlin to your home
It was hiding in my sack"

Chuck hugged the old elf
And whispered in his ear
"It's okay Santa
I'll love you always
Never, ever fear"

Santa said
"Thank you, Chuck
That's really very swell"
And then the old elf smiled real big and said
"I love you, as well"

Santa packed the dead gremlin up
And took it with him when he went
And in its place he left for Chuck
A very special present

Inside the gift a puppy waited to be found
When Chuck opened it and saw the dog
He could hardly make a sound

The dog bounded out immediately
And flew into Chuck's waiting arms
They fell together to the floor
But neither of them was harmed

The puppy licked Chuck's face
Chuck giggled happily
This was now the puppy's home
That was for sure
No such thing as probably

And they heard Santa call out
From where they sat on the floor
Santa said, "Merry Christmas, Chuck
Merry Christmas to all
And many, many more"

The Uglies

Ellie Evans gasped, startled at the sudden thud. She looked up to see yolk and shattered eggshell splattered against the large picture window, yellow *blood* dribbling down the glass. Another thud at the front door immediately followed. Then two more egg bombs exploded against the outside wall.

Maybe she shouldn't have come home from college; the Halloween tradition she dreaded most had already begun, and it wasn't even dusk yet.

"Gran," Ellie called. She threw her magazine onto the coffee table and jumped to her feet.

Another egg found the picture window, adding to the yellow and white carnage already defiling the glass.

"Witch…witch…witch…"

Along with the eggs, a chorus of catcalls bombarded the house now.

"Witch…witch…witch…"

"Gran!"

Ellie hurried to the front door, long, auburn curls flowing behind her, pretty, pale face set into a grim pose as if chiseled into place by a tormented sculptor. She reached for the doorknob but hesitated when an egg smashed against the other side.

Standing at the threshold, biting her lower lip until it bled, she anticipated the next round of egg bombs and listened to the unwarranted jeers outside her home.

"Stand aside, Ellie," Gran said.

As always, Ellie did as her grandmother instructed.

The old woman reached for the doorknob.

"Wait," Ellie warned, bringing her grandmother up short. "What if they still have eggs?"

Gran smiled but without humor. "It wouldn't be the first time I've been pelted with eggs…or worse." Loose strands of gray hair had escaped from the tight bun atop her head. She pushed them aside, revealing steely-blue eyes. "I must put a stop to this. I must remind everyone that we should be celebrated and not scorned. That we are all that stands between them and destruction."

"But they're just kids."

Gran nodded. "Kids repeating what they've heard at home." Her careworn face hardened. "Their parents and their grandparents have forgotten. They need reminding. Everyone needs reminding."

Without further argument, the old woman flung open the door. She stepped across the threshold and into the fray, undaunted by the taunts of the children and the eggs that splattered about her. She waved her frail arm as if it were a magic wand and cried, "Be gone."

The children scattered like autumn leaves in a bitter wind, accusations of witchery still on their lips but quickly dying with retreat.

The old woman charged across the porch but stopped short at the top of the steps. A groan escaped her lips as she clutched her left arm. Peering skyward, she saw black clouds forming on the horizon. A flash of light illuminated the oncoming blackness as she toppled down the stairs.

Ellie screamed. She took out her cell phone, dialing 911 as she rushed outside and across the porch to her grandmother. "I need an ambulance," she screeched into the phone.

The old woman reached out and dug long fingernails into her granddaughter's arm. "It's up to you now," she croaked, an edge of agony to her rusty voice. "If only your mother was still here."

"Gran," Ellie begged. "Don't leave me."

"It's up to you," Gran repeated, releasing her grip, hand flopping onto the ground.

"Gran," Ellie cried, tears bursting forth. She buried her face in her grandmother's bosom. "Don't leave me alone…"

But it did no good. And with the old woman's dying breath, the storm above gathered.

◆◆◆

On the outskirts of town, an ageless tree stood. Long, heavy branches reached out in all directions—leafless, gnarled and withered, bark peeling. An ugly, jagged scar marked the thick, twisted trunk where long ago there had once been a gaping wound. A small iron box was embedded within that scar, as if put there by magic.

Through the years, many strange tales swirled about town concerning the tree and the box—how the beautiful box came to be fixed within the tree trunk and the secrets the box held—each story more outlandish than the other, each varying in details, but each inevitably weaving itself back to the so-called witches who lived in town.

However, no one anymore truly feared the tree, the box, or any secrets they may have once held. Mostly, the tree had become a place where young people parked to be alone. A Ford Mustang was parked there now.

Overhead, the sky blackened. The atmosphere turned heavy, compressing the air below, a warning against the oncoming downpour still miles above the earth. A bolt of lightning ripped a hole through the surrounding blackness, ramming the iron box held captive within the tree. A thunderous boom followed in hot pursuit.

The Mustang shook from the nearby blast. The couple's embrace broke. They both stared at each other, wide-eyed and breathless.

"What was that?" Maggie whispered.

Luke used the palm of his hand to clear a fogged window. The squeal of his hand on glass raised the hackles on the back of Maggie's neck. They both pressed faces to the window.

Outside, storm clouds and dusk darkened the landscape. Lightning flashed on the horizon. Far off, thunder rumbled.

"Lightning must've hit the tree," Luke guessed.

The tree again had a gaping hole, the edges scorched. Smoke lingered in the heavy air. The iron box lay open a few feet from the base of the tree, blackened and smoldering, the secrets that had been hidden inside lost forever.

A small, dark figure, not more than four feet tall, staggered through the growing darkness and the lingering smoke.

"Someone's out there," Maggie exclaimed. "I

think it's a kid."

"It can't be a kid. What would a kid be doing out here all alone."

Maggie wiped away the returning fog, palm squealing against glass. "I tell you, it's a kid." She peered through the window. "We've gotta help him." She pounded Luke's shoulder with her fist. "Get out of the car. We've gotta help him."

"All right...stop hitting me."

Luke opened the door. The two scrambled out of the car but stopped short once outside.

A pungent odor of ozone hung in the still, heavy air. Lightning flashed, electricity igniting the night.

Luke and Maggie's hair stood on end. They held onto one another, neither of them sure now that getting out of the car was such a good idea.

The small, dark figure staggered toward them.

Maggie reached out a hand. "Don't be scared," she said. "We'll help you."

The figure stopped, answering Maggie with strange chittering sounds.

"Maggie, let's get back inside the car," Luke warned.

A second figure, just as small and dark, staggered out of the darkness. Another followed it, then another, more and more of them escaping through the gaping hole in the tree.

Chitter...chitter...chitter...

"Back inside the car," Luke repeated.

They stepped backwards, unwilling to turn their backs on these things.

The chittering grew louder and more rapid. Beady, red eyes blinked in the growing darkness. The leader exposed razor-sharp teeth and spread large, bat-like wings. The others followed suit.

Maggie screamed. Both she and Luke turned and ran toward the car. Luke tripped and fell. Maggie made it to safety within the Mustang, slamming the door behind her.

The horde shrieked in unison. They took flight, pouncing on their helpless prey.

Luke squealed. He kicked his legs, flailed his arms, but to no avail. There were too many. The things tore into him, ripping flesh and sucking blood. Soon his squeal died. His legs and arms only moved with involuntary spasms.

Witnessing the carnage, Maggie locked the doors and screeched in horror. She screeched again as more of the large, bat-like creatures pounced on the car, skittered across the hood, roof, and trunk, searching for a way inside. Ugly, rodent-like faces pressed against the glass, peering at her from all sides with their beady, red eyes. The constant chittering, the sounds of claws and wings scraping along the car, wracked Maggie's nerves. She eyed the ignition in hopes of finding the keys hanging there. They weren't; Luke must've taken them with him.

Maggie swallowed back burning bile and was considering her options when without warning the creatures took flight. She scanned the landscape and the sky the best she could, seeing no sign of the horrid beasts. When lightning flashed overhead what she did see was Luke, lying motionless on the ground. He had to have the keys. Steeling herself, she reached for the door. But before she could make her move, something rammed the car.

Maggie cried out, piercing and shrill, holding on

for dear life as time and again a large, winged creature dive-bombed her sanctuary, rocking it, denting it, cracking glass, until finally the windshield shattered and they were on her.

◆◆◆

Ellie sat on the sofa, tears and anguish marring her pretty face. Sobs choked her throat. Her hands fought with balled-up wads of Kleenex. Outside, lightning mixed with flashing red lights as the county coroner took away her grandmother's body.

Deputy-Sheriff James Steady sat on the sofa next to her. "I'm so sorry, El," he whispered.

A far-off peel of thunder answered.

Ellie stared at nothing, mute, trembling hands wrestling with the tissue.

"Those kids," the deputy continued, "they had no right taunting her the way they did, calling her a witch."

Ellie turned and eyed the man sitting next to her as if he were a stranger. But he was no stranger. The sight of his handsome face, brown eyes, and dark, wavy hair still made her heart jump just like when they dated in high school. "Jimmy," she said, "they had no right taunting her for what she was...but Gran was a witch." Choking back a sob, she pushed auburn curls from her face and wiped away tears.

Jim shook his head. "Don't talk like that, El. Your grandmother was a sweet old lady...nothing more."

Ellie squared her shoulders and gave the deputy a hard look. "Jim Steady, you know better. You didn't want to admit it to yourself when we dated in high school and apparently you still don't."

Jim looked away.

"It was the rumors that broke us up," Ellie insisted. "You didn't say so, but I knew it was true."

"El, I didn't—"

"It's okay," Ellie interrupted, "I understood…sort of." She shrugged. "But when you asked me out again, I assumed you'd come to terms with it." Now Ellie looked away. "I guess we should've talked about it before we made…" Her voice trailed off.

Jim reached for Ellie's hand.

She pulled it away.

"I hope you're not sorry," Jim whispered, "because I'm not."

Ellie looked Jim in the eye. "You're not sorry you love a witch?" she asked pointblank.

Before Jim could answer, what sounded like a sonic boom resounded through town and shook the small house.

Ellie jumped to her feet, ran to the window. "It's started," she cried.

Jim leapt up and followed, stopping behind her, peering through the window at the growing darkness. "What was that? What's started?"

Ellie didn't answer. "Take me to the tree," she said.

◆◆◆

Headlights on bright, spotlight lit, the police cruiser pulled up behind a wrecked vehicle.

Ellie gasped at the sight of the Ford Mustang: All four tires were flat. All the windows were shattered. The body of the car appeared to have been slammed repeatedly with a sledgehammer.

"My God," Jim exclaimed. "What happened?"

Ellie had no answer. Instead, she asked, "Can

you move the spotlight onto the tree?"

Jim did as she requested.

The tree had been split open, edges burned. A few feet away, a dark figure in ripped clothes was sprawled on the ground, looking like a discarded scarecrow, the stuffing stomped out of it. A few feet from that lay the iron box.

This confirmed Ellie's deepest fears; the death of her grandmother had broken the spell. "They're free," she murmured.

"I need to get out and investigate," Jim said, as if he hadn't heard Ellie's dreaded words. "El, I want you to stay put."

Ellie gathered herself, steeled her nerves. "Not on your life." She opened her door and climbed out.

Jim sighed, opened his door, and followed suit. They both first approached the stomped scarecrow. But the biting odor of death warned them that they wouldn't find remnants of straw.

Still, Ellie had to stifle a cry, the spotlight revealing every gory detail of the ravaged corpse. She held a hand over her mouth and nose, tears forming in her eyes as she watched flies and other bugs feed on what little flesh remained. "Who is it?" she choked.

The deputy shook his head. "Not enough left of him to tell. It looks as if animals have been feeding for days."

Ellie knew that nothing natural had done this and that it hadn't been days either.

Jim continued, "No one's filed a missing person's report recently, though."

This happened only thirty minutes ago, Ellie thought, *maybe less.* She scanned her surroundings,

43

fighting an instinctual urge to flee. She thought of warning Jim but decided he'd never believe her, not without evidence. So, for the time being, she kept quiet but alert.

Jim went to the Mustang, still illuminated within the police cruiser's headlights. He inspected the beaten car inside and out. "There's no one inside," he said, "but there's blood." He walked to the back of the Mustang and checked the license plate. "I'll run the number on the computer."

While Jim did that, Ellie stumbled to the tree, legs wobbly underneath her, still acutely aware that one or more of the things could still be hiding somewhere close. She examined the cavernous hole, glancing about with a nervous eye as she did so. Although seemingly impossible, the hole looked to go on forever—back and then down, as if it were a tunnel leading to perdition.

And maybe it was, Ellie thought, *for the things now loose upon this world were certainly born of the devil.*

Shivering, gooseflesh scampering across her skin like the bugs on that corpse, Ellie turned away. She tiptoed around the dead man—as if not to disturb his sleep—to the blackened and damaged iron box. It lay at her feet, opened and empty. She bent over to pick the box up but stopped short.

Chitter…chitter…

She stood, straining to hear, turning in circles, scanning her surroundings for the source of the strange noise. But she could see nothing lurking outside the light.

Then the noise stopped. In fact, the night had fallen deathly silent—no more thunder, no pitter-patter of raindrops, no insects, no night animals. The air hung heavy and still around her.

Chitter...chitter...

Ellie's breath caught in her throat. Her heart slammed against her ribcage. At least one of the escapees from the tree had remained behind. It now stalked her, she felt it. She glanced toward the police cruiser. Jim remained inside, safe. Continuing to scan her surroundings, she hunkered down and blindly picked up the iron box. She clutched it to her breast, stood, and crept toward the police cruiser, trying to remain at least outwardly calm.

Chitter...chitter...

A shadow moved across the lighted area as if a giant bird flew overhead.

Ellie dared not look skyward but could no longer pretend ignorance, could no longer maintain composure. A scream escaped her lips as she fled toward the car. Within only a few frantic steps, her stalker dropped out of the sky, pouncing on her as a hawk springs on a field mouse. Pain seized her neck and shoulder, sharp claws digging into her flesh. Crashing to the ground face first, a mouthful of dirt stifled her screams. She kicked and flailed as the thing dragged her along the ground.

Once outside the light, the thing collapsed on top of her. It folded its wings and wrapped them around her like a protective cocoon. But it offered no protection, only death as its dagger-like teeth ripped through her shirt and struck flesh.

In her mind, Ellie screamed and fought back. But in reality, with her face pressed into the dirt, with the thing weighing down on her and pinning her within its membranous wings, she couldn't

45

move or make a sound.

Muffled gunfire struck the night. On top of her, the thing convulsed. More gunfire followed. Teeth mercifully left her flesh. A shriek shattered her hearing. Wings released their grip. More gunfire hit the night. The thing rolled away, its shrieks turning to wails. One more shot and the night again fell deathly quiet and still.

Ellie raised her head, spitting and coughing up dirt. She rolled onto her back, tried to sit up. The pain pushed her back down. Clutching her neck and shoulder, her hand found wetness—warm and sticky.

"El," Jim hollered. He ran to her, squatted beside her, and helped her into a sitting position.

Ellie groaned and coughed. Although her hand still applied pressure to the wound, blood flowed freely through her fingers.

Jim brushed dirt-caked curls out of Ellie's face. Pulling a handkerchief from his pocket, he placed it over the wound.

Ellie winced.

"Sorry, I didn't mean to hurt you."

Ellie blinked away dirt. "You saved me."

Jim pulled the blood-soaked handkerchief away. "Not yet, we better get you to a hospital."

Ellie shook her head. "No."

"El, you could bleed to—"

"No," Ellie insisted. "Don't you have a first aid kit in the car?"

"Yeah, but—"

"Get it. Stop the bleeding."

Jim hurried off. He returned, setting the first aid kit on the ground. Hunkering down, he dressed the

46

wound. "What was that thing?"

Ellie flinched and grimaced. "An Ugly," she answered, seeing no reason to hold back, the proof of her claim lying dead just a few feet away. "At least that's what Gran called them."

Jim hesitated. He shook his head. "I've heard the story. But that's all it is—a scary story. There's no such thing." He finished and closed the kit.

"See for yourself," Ellie said. She put an arm around Jim's neck.

Jim stood, helping Ellie to her feet. Holding onto each other, they both stumbled toward the hideous corpse and the pool of blood that surrounded it.

"Does that look like just a story?"

Jim shivered at the sight. "Where'd it come from?"

Ellie shook her head. "I don't know. Gran didn't even know. They swooped out of the sky and attacked the town one night when Gran was just a girl. It was her mother's magic that imprisoned them in the tree."

"They? How many are there?"

"I don't know."

"How'd they get out? What happened to the magic spell?"

Ellie almost choked as she answered, "Gran died."

"But when your grandmother's mom died the magic still held."

"That's because by then Gran's magic was as strong as her mother's, and as her mother lay dying, Gran came to the tree and performed a ceremony. My mother should've been next in line to hold the magic spell."

"But she died when you were just a girl," Jim murmured.

Ellie nodded. She grimaced, pain shooting through her neck, throbbing into the back of her head. "And I was unprepared."

Jim pulled Ellie closer. "You can't blame yourself for your grandmother dying so suddenly."

"We should've been ready," Ellie explained, tears soaking her dirt-smudged face. "We weren't because college was more important to me than my craft or protecting the town."

Suddenly, the young woman's vision blurred. Her world spun. She barely kept her feet, leaning on Jim ever more heavily.

"We've got to get you to a doctor," Jim warned. "That bandage is almost soaked through. There must've been some kind of anticoagulant in that thing's saliva."

Ellie shook her aching head, pulled herself up straight, and steadied herself. "No time. I've got to put those things back."

"How?"

"I need the iron box."

"I'll get it." Cautiously, Jim released his grip.

Ellie swayed but remained standing as she waited.

When he returned, Jim asked, "Now what?"

"Now we need salt, holy water, and dirt from consecrated ground."

◆◆◆

After changing the blood-soaked bandage, the two raced off on their quest. Ellie's house was their first stop, where they were sure to find salt.

But they also found a town under siege. The

48

large, bat-like creatures bombarded houses—shattering windows, breaking down doors, crashing through roofs. People ran from their homes. Screams echoed through the streets. The creatures pounced on their prey. There was no place to hide. No one was safe.

Jim drove the police cruiser across the lawn, skidding to an abrupt stop in front of the porch. Grabbing the shotgun mounted to the dashboard, he pumped a round into the chamber. He took the pistol from his holster and held it out to Ellie. "I'll give you cover. Get inside…get the salt."

Ellie nodded. Reluctantly, she took the pistol, understanding the need to protect herself.

With the car still running, they both vaulted into the night. Ellie almost fell, somehow kept her feet. An Ugly swooped down. Jim opened fire, hitting it twice. The thing shrieked. It fell from the sky, a hard thud. Ellie staggered up the steps, into the house. She stumbled to the kitchen, gunfire outside booming much like the thunder had earlier. She found the salt easily enough, plus a small, glass vial, stuffing it into her pocket.

Retracing her steps, the house began to spin. Warm and wet, blood trickled down her back and her arm, the bandage no longer holding it at bay. Consciousness started slipping away. But somehow she managed to maneuver on unsteady feet to the front door.

Outside, war had broken out. Jim's shotgun boomed. More gunfire echoed throughout the town, other people having gotten out their guns and joining the battle.

But Ellie knew there were too many Uglies and

not enough townspeople with guns to kill all the foul things. She needed to hurry, despite weakening from loss of blood. Back at the car, she slumped in her seat, slamming the door.

Jim got off one more round before getting back behind the wheel. He reversed the car across the lawn and onto the street, tires squealing as they hit pavement. The tires squealed again as the car lurched forward, rocketing down the street in a cloud of smoke.

Sitting beside him, Ellie moaned.

"El, you okay?"

"Just drive," Ellie whispered. "Get me to the church."

They drove in silence, mesmerized by the pandemonium outside their windows. Gunfire still echoed in the night. But most people were just running for their lives. Winged creatures swooped out of the black sky, taking victims down, feeding at will.

Jim hit the gas. With emergency lights flashing, the police cruiser zoomed down the street, swerving around fleeing pedestrians and speeding cars alike. When the car skidded to a stop outside the church, Jim grabbed the shotgun. He loaded shells and pumped a round into the chamber. "Let's do it," he said.

They both immediately hurled themselves into harm's way. Jim's shotgun boomed. Ellie clutched the pistol in her blood-drenched hand as she hurried up the church steps. Pure adrenaline kept her conscious, kept her moving. She rushed through the door, pulled out the vial, and immersed it into holy water.

But as she capped the vial and turned to leave, she heard that same awful sound she'd heard out by the tree, before being attacked.

Chitter...chitter...

She whirled around, brought the pistol up, blindly fired. The report echoed through the church. The recoil almost knocked her off her feet. She screamed in pain. Blood dribbled from her gun hand to the floor.

The thing scrambling toward her shrieked. Blood gushed from its chest. It stumbled in its advance but kept coming.

Ellie braced herself, took better aim, and fired. Her own scream of pain equaled the creature's wail. But in the end Ellie remained standing. The Ugly lay dead in the aisle.

Ellie turned away, staggering from the church. She made it down the steps and collapsed onto the pavement.

"El, hurry," Jim hollered, shotgun booming.

Ellie climbed to her feet, the world around her spinning, her mind swimming. She shuffled to the car, fell into it, and slammed the door.

Jim jumped in next. The car rocketed away, swerving, tires squealing.

Ellie closed her eyes and trusted herself to the deputy's driving skills. Consciousness fought her every second of the way. Drifting in and out, aware but not aware, the world around her was nothing but loud noises and darkness. Before she knew it, the car lurched to an abrupt stop.

"El, we're here." Jim gave her a gentle nudge.

Ellie moaned. Opening her eyes, her blurred vision focused on Jim, noticing the nasty gash across his forehead. "You okay?" she whispered.

Jim didn't answer. Instead he said, "I better change that bandage."

Ellie nodded. "Jimmy, do it fast. We're running out of time."

Jim retrieved the first aid kit. He cleaned and dressed the wound the best he could. "El, you stay put and let me get the dirt."

"No—"

"El, you need to save your strength for the ceremony." Jim turned on the spotlight and scanned the graveyard. "There's no sign of the creatures. I'll only be a minute."

Ellie knew she should finish the task herself. She knew she shouldn't let Jim go in her stead. But he was right. She needed to conserve energy. The ceremony would take all her strength. "Okay," she agreed, "but be careful. Take the iron box. Fill it about a third full."

Jim grabbed the box. "Be right back. You hang on, El. We're almost finished." He climbed out of the car, took three steps toward the cemetery, and froze.

Chitter…chitter…

It came from behind. He whirled toward the sound.

One of the horrid creatures perched itself on the roof of the police cruiser. It shrieked and spread bat-like wings.

Jim reached for his holster. Empty; he'd given the pistol to Ellie and foolishly left the shotgun in the car.

Razor-sharp teeth bared, the Ugly launched itself at Jim. Both man and beast hit the ground as one.

52

The creature wrapped wings around its prey, ripped into flesh, feasted on free-flowing blood.

The commotion outside the car woke Ellie from a semiconscious state. She jerked upright, scanning her surroundings. Within the harsh glare of the spotlight, she saw Jim and one of the creatures in mortal combat.

"Jimmy!" Ellie screamed.

Adrenalin shot through her. She scrambled out of the car. Clutching the pistol in her sticky, blood-stained hand, she ran toward the battle. She fired, screaming in both pain and horror. She hit the thing square in the back, but it refused to release its hold on Jim. Skidding to a stop over the two combatants, she took careful aim and again fired. The creature's head blew apart, skull cracking open like an egg, gory yolk of brain tissue and blood splattering the air and ground.

With her foot, Ellie shoved the thing away. She hunkered down, desperate to see Jim's handsome face. But what she saw sickened her. She turned away, retching and heaving. After emptying her insides, she dared not look again but forced herself to check for a pulse. She found none.

The iron box rested a few feet from the dead. Ellie choked back her grief, wiping away tears as she stood. Scooping up the box, she stumbled through the cemetery, determined to complete the mission. At a gravesite, she dropped to her knees and clawed with her fingers at the sod, dumping into the box clumps of hallowed ground.

◆◆◆

The police cruiser crashed into the banged-up Mustang. Ellie spilled out. She staggered toward the tree, dropped to her knees, and laid out everything in front of her. She first poured a ring of salt around herself for protection. After opening the iron box, she poured the remaining salt in with the sacred dirt.

She chanted, *"Aboon dabashmaya, nethkadash shamak. Tetha malkoothak. Newe tzevyanak aykan dabashmaya."*

Overhead, lightning flashed. Thunder boomed.

She poured in the holy water then slammed the lid shut.

"Af bara hav lan lakma dsoonkanan. Yamana washbook lan kavine aykana daf."

Nature's strobe light lit the night sky. Rapid-fire thunder bombs exploded all around. A multitude of shrieks echoed above it all. The swarm of Uglies covered the night sky like fast-moving storm clouds.

Bleeding, barely hanging onto life, Ellie raised both arms to the heavens. *"Hanan shabookan lhayavine oolow talahn lanesyana. Ela fatsan men beesha."*

With that, the swarm dive-bombed past her like guided missiles, back through the cavernous hole in the tree from hence they came. When the last of the horrid creatures entered the hollow tree, Ellie picked up the iron box and threw it after them. The tree miraculously healed itself, a scar appearing where seconds ago there'd been a gaping hole. Embedded in that scar was the iron box.

Ellie collapsed, everything going black.

◆◆◆

Twenty years later, Ellie lay dying, riddled with cancer. Her daughter Jamie sat at her bedside, keeping vigil.

"Jamie," Ellie croaked, "there's not much

time…go to the tree…perform the ceremony."

Jamie pushed back auburn curls and wiped away free-flowing tears. "I want to stay here with you, Mama."

"You must be strong, Jamie. Go to the tree now, before it's too late."

Jamie stood. "I love you, Mama."

Ellie gazed into her daughter's face for the last time. "I love you, dear. Now go, make your father and me proud."

Jamie turned away, rushing outside to her destiny.

Black storm clouds gathered overhead. Lightning flashed. Thunder rumbled. On the outskirts of town, the tree stood, withered and twisted.

And the Uglies waited for another chance at freedom.

Fred Wiehe

Raven Mocker

Dry cackles echoed through the graveyard.

Charlie Two-Lives stared up into the surrounding trees. The old man's withered hand gripped the head of his cane with white-knuckled intensity as he watched large, crow-like birds gather on the branches overhead. Why his grandson Jimmy—who stood by him at the graveside—paid them no mind he couldn't figure. Maybe Jimmy mistook the raspy caws as nothing more than nature's funeral dirge for Charlie's fallen friend.

But Charlie knew better. The birds weren't there to pay respects. They were there to mock the dead and the dying.

Jimmy cleared his throat. He gave Charlie a solemn look and said, "The funeral was a great mix of Christian and Cherokee, don't you think?"

Charlie didn't respond. Instead, he lost himself in the wicked and raucous chorus coming from above him.

"Don't you think?" Jimmy asked, trying again to engage his stoic grandfather.

Charlie stared into the trees rather than down at the casket in the open grave. He uttered not a word or sound.

He again wondered why his grandson paid the

57

birds no mind. Maybe Jimmy couldn't see or hear them at all. That must be it. The large, black birds were there for Charlie alone. His time must be near, for he had seen and heard a gathering flock such as this once before, the first time he had faced death, almost forty years ago.

"Grandfather," Jimmy prompted, "everyone else has gone."

Not taking the hint, Charlie remained mute and rooted.

Jimmy sighed, resigned to his grandfather's stubborn ways. "I still don't understand who would want to harm Ben," he said, trying a new tact to engage Charlie. "He was an old man," Jimmy continued, eyeing his grandfather. "Besides that, he was dirt poor. Why would anyone break into his home and do...what they did to him?"

Charlie shook his head. A tear meandered down his cheek. He had been the one to find his friend's broken and beaten body. The reservation police had insisted it was a robbery gone wrong, that someone had used a pickax to gain entry through the front door, and then to their surprise found Ben at home and killed him. But that couldn't explain why the culprit desecrated Ben's already crumpled, dead body by slicing him open and removing his heart, lungs, and liver. That didn't explain the large, black feathers scattered on the floor around the body.

No, it was not a robbery gone wrong. Final proof of that was this gathering of phantom birds at Ben's grave sight.

"Kalona," Charlie whispered.

Jimmy eyed the old man. "What, Grandfather?" he asked. "You know my Cherokee is none too

58

good."

Charlie turned to his grandson and smiled. "Everyone else has gone," he said. "Why aren't we?"

Jimmy shook his head and sighed. Then, in spite of himself, he broke into a grin. "I guess I was holding things up, Grandfather. I never know when to shut up."

With that, they turned to leave, the raucous caws of the black birds chasing after them as they made their way around the crumbling tombstones and through the rusted gate of the old cemetery.

They climbed into Jimmy's Ford pickup and drove the long expressway across the reservation, back toward Charlie's decrepit shack. In the distance, they could see the *Rocky Road Cherokee Casino*, a behemoth, pristine building, out of place in the surrounding poverty, as if alien spaceships had beamed it up and transported it to a third world country. Rich people came and went everyday, driving the same road in their BMWs and Mercedes, going to gamble their money away, barely noticing the ramshackle buildings, rusted-out automobiles, and dirty, barefoot children outside their windows.

Jimmy cleared his throat. "Grandfather, have you thought anymore about coming to live with me in town?"

Charlie looked out the window and shook his head.

"I would take good care of you...Lisa too," Jimmy insisted. "You could be happy there if you gave it a chance."

They turned off the paved expressway, onto a dirt road. Slowly, the truck bumped along, kicking up pebbles and dust for two miles, before pulling up outside Charlie's place. The small shack stood in a stand of oak trees, half-hidden from the road, no other house around for a good five miles.

"Grandfather, I'm worried about you," Jimmy persisted. "What would you do way out here if you needed help? I'm sorry, but you're not getting any younger. You don't drive anymore. You don't have a phone. Now some madman is going around breaking into homes and mutilating people. I don't want you to end up like poor, old Ben."

Charlie looked at his grandson with deep affection. He said, "I have lived my whole life on the Res. I will die on the Res." He reached over and squeezed Jimmy's arm. "Living in town will not save me from what killed Ben, my grandson."

"What does that mean?"

"The Kalona will find me wherever I go."

"I don't understand. What's a…Kalona?"

"A Raven Mocker…a demon…an old nemesis."

Jimmy's jaw dropped. He chuckled but without humor. "You're talking about some old Cherokee myth…Raven Mockers…specters of the undead…like in some cheap Hollywood movie…if it were made by Indians. It's nonsense."

"You did not see the phantom birds in the graveyard. You did not hear their unearthly caws. I did, as I saw and heard them over forty years ago in my other life."

Jimmy shook his head. Three times, he pounded his open palm against the steering wheel, frustrated by old Cherokee beliefs that had no place in the modern world. "When is your generation going to let go of the old beliefs? It's the twenty-first

60

century, for God's sake."

"The century does not matter, my grandson," Charlie explained. "The Raven Mocker has existed for as long as man has walked the earth. It is drawn to those on the verge of death. Only their next victim can see the signs, can see them coming. It renews its life force by drinking the blood or devouring the entrails of the living. But in its blackened heart it is a coward, so it preys only on the old and the dying. My time surely is near. My second life must almost be over."

"This is crazy, Grandfather," Jimmy insisted. He gripped the steering wheel with both hands as if it were a lifeline to sanity. Then suddenly the last thing his grandfather had said hit him. "What do you mean...your second life is almost over? What second life?"

"It is how I came by the name Two-Lives, my grandson," Charlie explained with patience only possessed by the old and the wise.

"What?"

"Forty years ago I had faced death, lost in the wilderness, my leg broken and dragging behind me. I desperately crawled back down the mountain, but I neared death faster than salvation. That's when the crow-like birds gathered in the trees and surrounded me, as they had this morning in the graveyard."

"There were no birds in the graveyard," Jimmy argued, now squeezing the steering wheel in a death grip.

Charlie ignored the interruption. He continued, "Next came the Raven Mocker, manifesting as a giant, terrifying bird, its wings outstretched and outlined with flickering tongues of fire. It screeched

61

and came at me hard, hideous beak ripping into my flesh. But I was not as near death as it had hoped and stronger than it had expected. As we rolled along the ground, in mortal combat, I pulled the Bowie knife from my boot and planted it in the thing's chest. Shrieking with pain, the coward fled into the sky, the flock of birds following close behind. Like storm clouds, they blocked the sun and blackened the sky, until finally disappearing from sight. I continued down the mountain, broken and bleeding. But somehow I survived. Ben and some others found me in the foothills. They brought me home, and I began my second life."

Jimmy tried to remain calm. "Grandfather, you were hurting, bleeding, probably dehydrated and in shock too. Obviously, you were hallucinating. There's no such thing as a Raven Mocker."

Charlie stared straight ahead, unflinching, secure in his knowledge that the Raven Mocker was not a hallucination.

Jimmy released his death grip on the steering wheel. "I'm not going to lose you too," he whispered. Turning toward Charlie, he scrutinized the old man's stoic profile. "Tomorrow you're moving into town. No arguments. I'll take care of you, and Lisa will help best she can. You pack everything up tonight. Be ready to go in the morning."

"You are treating me like a child."

"You're acting like a child," Jimmy scolded. "Your friend's dead, murdered by some madman, and you're talking crazy about a legend told to scare little children at night."

Charlie opened the truck's door and climbed out,

leaning against his cane.

"I mean it," Jimmy persisted, "pack tonight. Be ready to move into town tomorrow morning."

Charlie slammed the door. He turned and walked away, cane in hand, moving slowly toward his shack.

The truck pulled away, kicking up dirt and pebbles as if manifesting its driver's anger, finally retreating into the distance in a cloud of dust.

Inside, Charlie readied himself, not for moving into town but for doing battle with the Raven Mocker. He was old and resigned to dying, but after all these years he wasn't about to let his old nemesis rip him apart and feast on his insides. The thought of it sickened him, and he refused to go to his third life that way. Hopefully, he still had enough strength and vigor to fight off the foul thing one last time.

Taking the Winchester down from over the fireplace, Charlie loaded it for the first time in years. From his sock drawer, he took the same Bowie knife he had plunged into the Raven Mocker's breast forty years ago. He stuck that in his boot. He maneuvered his favorite chair to the center of the room and sat down, facing the door. His cane went on the floor. The rifle rested in his lap. There was nothing for him to do now but wait. As time passed, his thoughts drifted, and his eyes grew heavy and closed.

A roar not unlike a mountain lion jolted him out of a dreamless sleep. The squeal of pigs being slaughtered quickly followed. It didn't sound like the prelude he expected to the Raven Mocker's attack. Still, although groggy with sleep, he aimed the rifle at the door, readying himself for anything.

Outside, dusk crept along the landscape and pressed against the windows. Inside, dark shadows lurked in every corner.

Charlie hid in those shadows, waiting for the imminent attack, dry mouth choking him as no two hands could. Sweat beaded on his brow, trickled down his face, along his neck and throat, and under his shirt. The Winchester shook in his damp, slippery grasp.

Still, he waited.

But instead of the Raven Mocker attacking, slamming car doors assaulted the night.

He lowered the rifle, slowly understanding, relief overtaking him. Coming out of a deep sleep, groggy and confused, he had mistaken the roar of an engine for a wild animal. The squeal he now realized was the familiar sound from the shoddy brakes on Jimmy's truck.

Instead of the Raven Mocker, his grandson had come for him.

Sure enough, his grandson opened the door and stood framed in the doorway. "Grandfather?" called Jimmy.

"I am here," Charlie answered.

"Why are you sitting here in the dark?"

Jimmy crossed the room and turned on a lamp. The light immediately beat the shadows back into the far side of the room.

"And what's with the rifle?"

"It's for the—"

"Don't tell me," Jimmy interrupted, "it's for the Raven Mocker."

"Yes. Why are you here?"

"Lisa convinced me that you shouldn't be alone.

I told her your story about the Raven Mocker, and she persuaded me to come get you tonight rather than wait until morning. This proves she was right." Jimmy took the Winchester from his grandfather. He placed it back on the rack over the fireplace. "You could've killed someone, Grandfather."

"Jimmy, aren't you glad you listened to me now?" Lisa asked, framed in the doorway.

"Lisa," Charlie whispered. In all the confusion, he hadn't noticed the girl until that moment. He picked up his cane, stood on shaky legs, and went to his grandson's wife. "You don't look well," he said.

"Grandfather, I'm fine," Lisa insisted.

"No, come and sit down."

Charlie led the thin, frail girl back to the chair and helped her sit.

Jimmy stood at Charlie's side.

"She doesn't look well, Jimmy," Charlie repeated. "She is pale and weak."

Jimmy shuffled his feet.

"Tell him," Lisa said. She hid her face in her hands and began to sob.

"What?" Charlie asked.

Jimmy looked at his feet. "It's true, Grandfather...Lisa's not well," he choked. "She has...cancer. We didn't want to worry you."

"Cancer," Charlie spat out the word like a piece of rancid meat.

Lisa choked back her sobs. She looked up and dried her eyes. "This changes nothing," she insisted.

"That's right," Jimmy agreed. "You're still coming to live with us. We can still take care of you."

"Cancer," Charlie repeated.

His physical eyes went vacant, but his mind's eye finally saw everything clearly. The crow-like birds hadn't been at the graveyard for him; although old, he was still in good health. They had been there because of Lisa. They had smelled Lisa's death scent on Jimmy. That's what had attracted them.

Wings fluttered nearby. A scratchy cackle shattered the night.

"What was that?" Lisa asked.

"What was what? I didn't hear anything," Jimmy said.

Charlie turned to Lisa. "You heard it too?"

Eyes wide, she nodded in response.

The beating of wings and incessant, dry raspy shrieks now surrounded the shack, sounding as if a hundred birds battled just outside its walls.

"It's coming," Charlie yelled.

"What's coming?" Jimmy asked. He moved in front of Charlie and grabbed the old man by the arms, steadying him. "Stay calm. What's coming?"

A large, black bird crashed against the window. Another followed in its wake, shattering the pane. Deafening thuds pounded the shack all around them, hundreds of birds flying into the walls.

Lisa screamed.

Charlie dropped his cane. "It's coming," he yelled again. With a strength he hadn't realized he still possessed, he threw Jimmy aside.

Jimmy fell into a table, hit his head, and both he and table crashed to the floor.

Lisa jumped to her feet and screamed again.

Charlie rushed the door. Slammed it shut. Locked it.

A shiny, black beak punched a hole right

through it.

Quickly, Charlie backed away, almost tripping over Jimmy lying unconscious on the floor. The old man pulled the Bowie knife from his boot and held a screaming Lisa to his side in a protective embrace.

Again and again, the foot-long beak hammered the door, ripping it to splinters. Soon the Raven Mocker filled the doorway, its beady eyes black onyx, its obsidian feathers adorned with sparkles of fiery light. The giant bird crossed the threshold, talons ticking against the wooden floor.

The sight of the foul thing silenced Lisa into a catatonic state. Charlie lowered the girl back into the chair. He brandished the Bowie knife out in front of him—he, an old man, the only thing standing between the sick girl and certain death. He wished he had the Winchester, but Jimmy had taken it from him and had hung it back on the wall. By the time he got to it, the Raven Mocker could easily rip Lisa to shreds. Charlie's only hope was to stand his ground.

"You want her," Charlie taunted, "you must again face me, Kalona."

The Raven Mocker screeched murderously and attacked.

Charlie slashed at it, the blade of his knife finding a large, outstretched wing. But the demon's beak too found its mark, ripping into Charlie's face. Charlie slashed the blade of his knife across the thing's breast even as he himself cried out in pain.

The Raven Mocker staggered backwards, talons ticking, shrieking with both pain and homicidal intent. It lunged again, grabbing Charlie by his shirt with its beak.

Being lifted off the floor, Charlie found the scar on the Raven Mocker's breast from the wound he had inflicted upon the foul thing forty years ago. He plunged the Bowie knife deep into that scar.

A second later, the giant bird flicked its head and sent the old man crashing into the wall. On impact, the sickening sound of cracking bones filled Charlie's ears. He gasped and groaned, landing in a broken heap, breathing labored, blood trickling from his mouth.

The Raven Mocker's hideous screech and Lisa's torturous screams were the last things Charlie heard before everything went pitch black.

◆◆◆

Six months later, Charlie sat in the reservation jailhouse, awaiting trial. His physical injuries had healed, and they had released him from the hospital. But mentally and emotionally he still felt dazed and confused, even after so much time had passed, even after being questioned to death by both police and court-appointed shrinks, even after telling his story over and over again. But the more he told it, the more no one really listened.

With each retelling, even he began to doubt his own innocence, his own sanity.

Sitting on the bunk in his cell, Charlie wrung his sweaty hands together and stared at the concrete floor. "I have killed no one," he mumbled. "I was only trying to save her...only trying to save her. I have killed no one."

How could Jimmy believe it? How could anyone believe it?

Tears welled in the old man's eyes. He shook his head and buried his face in his hands. "I loved her

68

like a daughter. I have killed no one."

But Jimmy thought he had. The police thought he had. They thought he had rendered Jimmy unconscious and in a fit of madness sliced poor Lisa open with his Bowie knife. They thought he had cut her entrails out and eaten them. They thought he had killed Ben too.

"I am Charlie Two-Lives," he sobbed, "I have killed no one."

But no one listened anymore. No one believed in the Raven Mocker. No one cared about the splintered front door, even though no pickax was found. No one gave much thought to the large, black feathers that had surrounded both Ben and Lisa's remains.

"I am Charlie Two-Lives," he sobbed. "I have killed no one."

Dry cackles echoed outside his cell, like demonic laughter.

Charlie startled at the sound. He stood, wiping tears from his eyes as he limped to the cell window.

Outside, hundreds of large, crow-like birds gathered in the trees. Their raucous refrain taunted him, mocked him.

Charlie gripped the window bars, white-knuckled. "I am Charlie Two-Lives," he screamed through the bars. "I have killed no one."

But even the birds wouldn't listen.

Fred Wiehe

Santa's War

Outside, monster currents of wind kicked swirls of already fallen snow into the air as if trying to return the white stuff back to the heavens. Trees bent to the ground against the will of the blustery weather. The small house groaned with displeasure. Windows rattled, fighting against the brute force. One double-framed window lost the battle, flying open, smashing against both sides of the inside wall. The monster wind charged through the opening. With it, came a crumpled piece of paper.

Santa rushed to the beaten window, boots crunching broken glass underfoot. In the face of the wind, the old man's long, white hair and beard whipped into tangled messes. He forced both sides of the window frame shut, but the wind still rushed through gaping holes of missing panes. He turned away to find boards and tools to fix the problem but stopped short at the sight of the crumpled paper that rested on the floor amongst the tiny shards of glass. After picking the paper up, he smoothed it out and glanced at the writing. It was a letter, and the first few words set his hands to trembling and his heart to thudding:

71

Dear Santa,

I need help! Mom is dead. I think Dad killed her. Or something pretending to be my dad did anyway. Like, I don't know. He scares me. I locked myself in my room. He wants to kill me too. I'm sure.

I'm eleven and like stopped believing in you a couple years ago. But I have no where else to turn, okay. The phone is broke. The Internet's down. I hope I'm wrong, and you're like...real...or something. I hope you get this. Come quick.

Help! Please!
Bobby Wetrz
1512 Hunt Road
Reading, Ohio

Santa read the letter three times. Each time his heart raced faster. Blood pounded in his ears, muffling the eerie whistle of the monstrous wind swirling about him.

Could this be a hoax of some sort? Where'd the letter come from? Could the wind have brought the letter, delivering it like an invisible postal worker?

There were too many unanswered questions. There were too many coincidences. But how could he just ignore the bizarre letter? He couldn't. A child's life might truly be at stake.

An elf burst into the room. "Santa, we're burning the Eve," Gideon chimed, "the team's hitched and ready—" The elf's words choked in his throat when first he saw the broken window and then the horrified expression on Santa's face. "Whoa," he said, "what's happened?"

Santa didn't answer, dumbstruck by the letter.

"Santa?" prompted Gideon.

Santa stuffed the letter into a pocket of his red coat. Rushing past the elf, he said, "Let's go. Like you said, Gideon, we're burning the Eve, and we've got a lot of stops to make."

Gideon turned, hot on Santa's tail. He followed his boss across the house and outside to the waiting sleigh. The reindeer snorted and stomped their hooves in the snow with anticipation of the long night's work ahead. The wind bit into Santa's face and tossed his hair and beard about as he climbed into the sleigh. Gideon hopped in behind him. Santa picked up the reins, giving them a good shake. Jingle bells rang out. Without a verbal command, the team of reindeer took flight. Off they went into what was supposed to be the happiest and most exciting night of the year, delivering presents around the world to deserving girls and boys.

Only Santa knew of the possible impending dangers ahead.

The route they took that night was not their usual one. But neither elf nor reindeer questioned Santa's purpose for altering plans and heading first to the small town of Reading, Ohio. Soon, the reindeer and sleigh settled softly onto the roof of 1512 Hunt Road.

With some hesitation, Santa climbed out of the sleigh. He planted heavy boots onto the snow-laden roof then reached for his magic bag and slung it over his shoulder.

Gideon made a move to follow.

"You stay with the team, Gideon," Santa ordered.

Gideon sat down hard, a look of dejection

twisting the tiny features of his face.

Santa patted the elf on the shoulder. "It's best this way," he said. Sweat gleamed across the old man's face, despite the bitter cold.

Gideon's expression turned from dejection to worry. "What aren't you telling me, Santa?" he asked.

Santa shivered, fear and winter cold both grabbing hold. "Better you not know," he said. "Stay with the team. Don't come in, no matter what."

Gideon eyed his boss, concern etched across his small face. "Santa—"

"No matter what, Gideon," Santa interrupted. "Promise me."

Gideon nodded. "I promise, Santa."

Santa turned away, heading for the chimney. He climbed into the opening and stared back at the frightened elf. He wished he could say something to ease Gideon's mind, to calm the poor elf. But there was nothing to say. Santa himself had no idea what dangers waited within the house. How could he relieve someone else's fear when terror gripped his own heart like the cold hand of death?

So without saying a word, he slid down the chimney into the unknown.

Santa landed with a thud in the fireplace. With the magic bag slung over his shoulder, he ventured out into the room. He could see very little, his eyes not yet adjusted to the surrounding darkness. Yet even over the nervous thumping of reindeer hooves on the roof above, he could hear a strange slurping noise coming from somewhere in the room. He sniffed the air, almost gagging on the sickening-sweet odor permeating it.

What in God's name was he getting himself into?

Santa almost called out to Bobby but thought better of it. Instead, with a hand out in front of him, he moved cautiously forward through the darkness, unconsciously moving toward the source of the slurping sound and the terrible smell. But before he got very far, the overhead lights switched on. A harsh brightness now surrounded him.

"Stop, Santa!"

From behind, a boy hollered. But Santa didn't turn around. Instead, he squinted at the horrible sight ahead.

A dead woman lay splayed on the floor, her stomach split open, intestines and organs spilling out. A man knelt nearby in a pool of blood. He lapped up the red stuff like a dog at a water bowl.

"My God," Santa muttered.

In response, the man looked up with a blood-smeared face. He growled and bared teeth, no longer truly a man, now nothing more than a rabid animal or maybe a zombie like in a cheesy horror movie.

"Run, Santa!"

Santa turned toward the screaming boy.

Bobby stood at the top of a staircase, his hand poised on a light switch. "Santa, run," he hollered again.

But Santa didn't move. Instead, he turned back to the bloody mess. Fear froze him.

The monstrous man now stood on wobbly legs. He shuffled forward, snarling and growling, reaching for the bearded man in the red suit.

Santa somehow shook free of his fear. He

dropped his bag. From within it, he pulled out a Glock 21. He blasted Bobby's former dad with six rounds from the .45 caliber pistol, hitting the advancing monster each time in the chest.

From behind, Bobby screamed.

The man staggered backward. Blood spurted from his wounds. But he didn't stop. He came at Santa again, stiff and rigid like Frankenstein's monster, upper lip curled back in a snarl, bloodstained teeth bared. With unsatisfied hunger, he groaned and reached for his prey.

Santa backed up toward the staircase. He opened fire again. The report of the large handgun echoed throughout the house, joining Bobby's steady scream.

As each bullet hit its mark, the man jerked and flung about like a marionette being controlled by a mad puppeteer. Tiny geysers of blood spurted from multiple wounds.

Santa kept pulling the trigger, emptying the thirteen-round magazine into his adversary. But the man or zombie or monster or whatever only swayed on his feet rather than dropping dead to the floor.

"Santa, come on," Bobby hollered. The boy had stopped screaming and somehow found the courage to come down the stairs. He now tugged on Santa's red coat. "Please, come on," he begged.

Santa dropped the now empty and useless handgun. But he couldn't move because the sight of what happened next mesmerized and horrified him all the more.

The bullet-riddled zombie-monster-man's chest split open. Flesh ripped. Bones cracked. Along with body organs and fluid, the true monster came slithering out of the gaping wound, slimy and slippery, multiple squid-like tentacles reaching out in all directions. The large, alien-looking thing plopped onto the floor as its dead host fell backwards with a loud thud.

The beast or alien skittered across the floor toward Santa and Bobby. Its huge, horrid mouth opened, exposing rows of shark-like teeth.

Was it looking for a meal or a new host to do its bidding?

Either way, Santa wanted no part of it. He again reached into his magic bag. This time, he pulled out an M16A1 Assault Rifle. He felt Bobby tug on his coat again.

"Come on," Bobby screamed. He stopped tugging on Santa's coat and retreated back up the stairs.

Santa grabbed his bag and tossed it over his shoulder, onto the stairs. "Take this with you, Bobby," he yelled.

Bobby thumped back down the stairs, stopped, and then dragged the heavy bag back up to the landing.

Santa backpedaled up one step and then another. As he moved, he locked down the rifles bolt and pushed the bolt carrier into its forward-most position.

Meanwhile, the alien beast kept advancing. It skittered forward with tentacles flailing, leaving a snail-like, slimy trail in its wake.

Santa opened fire. At first he started out with three-round blasts. But quickly he switched to full auto capability. Explosions of gunfire resounded repeatedly throughout the house. Spent shell casings clanked to the floor. Gun smoke choked the air. The assault rifle felt so hot he almost dropped it. But he didn't. He kept firing—thirty rounds directly into the attacking alien.

But the beast didn't die or even stop. Instead, with each shot that hit it, the thing split off and mutated into a smaller duplicate of itself. Soon, instead of one horrible alien to defeat, there were ten then twenty then thirty.

Santa backed up two more steps. He yelled, "Bobby, throw me another magazine."

Bobby searched the magic bag. He found the clip and tossed it down to Santa.

Santa detached the empty magazine, caught the new one, and slammed it into place in one swift motion. By now he was surrounded. With the horrible beasts almost on top of him, Santa sprayed them with bullets.

But each time a round ripped into a little beast, it again duplicated. Soon sixty or more smaller but just as vicious aliens came skittering across the floor. The beasties were now at the bottom of the stairs, using their tentacles to pull themselves up.

The rifle became too hot to handle. With his ears ringing from gunfire, Santa threw the weapon aside and dashed up the steps to Bobby.

Gideon landed hard on his butt in the fireplace. "Santa," he yelled. The elf struggled to his feet and without thinking ran into the fray. "I'll help you."

"Gideon, go back," Santa shouted.

It was too late. The aliens turned as if they had one mind, attacking the courageous yet defenseless elf. A slithering mass of slimy bodies and slashing tentacles were quickly on their prey, mouths snapping, teeth ripping and rending flesh.

Gideon's scream came from somewhere underneath the pile, but neither Santa nor Bobby could see any sign of their would-be rescuer.

"Gideon," Santa bellowed. He made a move to help his friend, but Bobby grabbed the back of the old man's coat.

"No, Santa…it's like too late."

Santa stopped.

Bobby was right. There was no saving the elf. But maybe Gideon hadn't died in vain. Maybe he had bought the time needed for Bobby and Santa to escape.

Santa grabbed his magic bag. "Let's get to your room, Bobby."

Bobby took Santa's hand and led the way down a hall. They stopped outside a closed door. On the door was a sign that read:

Bobby's Room
KEEP OUT!

Santa doubted that those things would heed that warning. "Hurry, Bobby," he said.

As Bobby opened the door, the two rushed inside. Santa slammed the door shut and raced to the window. Iron bars were bolted to the outside wall, making the room a prison. Santa gave Bobby a disappointed and quizzical look.

Bobby shrugged. "Mom and Dad," he began, choking up, wiping tears away, "were like worriers, you know. They thought someone might…you know…get in…like kidnap me or something."

Santa patted the boy's head.

"Oh, Santa," Bobby wailed. With all his might, he hugged the old man. "Why did this happen? What are we gonna do?" He buried his face in Santa's fat belly and sobbed.

Santa hugged the boy back. "I'm sorry about your parents, Bobby. I don't know why this happened." He looked about the room. "But I do know that we're going to make a stand right here. Don't give up just yet."

Bobby peered up at Santa with a hopeful expression.

"When we get out of this Bobby, you're coming to live with me at the North Pole, okay?"

Bobby wiped away tears, sniffed back snot, and nodded.

Santa smiled and winked at the boy.

Loud thuds at the door brought the two back to reality and their perilous situation. The things had finished their appetizer downstairs and were now on the threshold of Bobby's room for the main dish.

Santa thought about barricading the door with Bobby's dresser or bed but reconsidered; it would only prolong the inevitable because sooner or later the alien creatures would burst through or find a way inside.

Santa had other plans instead. "Get behind me, Bobby," he said.

Bobby obeyed, squeezing between Santa's wide back and the wall behind.

Reaching into his magic bag, Santa pulled out a handheld flamethrower. He strapped on the backpack containing three cylinder tanks—the two outside tanks filled with a flammable, oil-based liquid fuel and the middle tank filled with a flammable, compressed gas. A fuel hose and a gas pipe ran from the tanks to the gun housing that he now held firmly in his trembling hands.

The thuds at the door grew louder and closer together, sounding similar to the rapid-fire of an automatic weapon; the alien creatures apparently were throwing themselves against the door in their attempt to get inside. And it was working. The doorjamb began to splinter and crack, ready to give way.

To prepare the flamethrower, Santa opened the ignition valve and pressed a button that activated the two spark plugs positioned in front of the gun's nozzle. This created a small flame. He was now ready to shoot deadly fire streams.

The door to Bobby's room burst open. Shrapnel of splintered wood flew about. The slimy beasts swarmed into the room, tentacles flailing, mouths snapping. They skittered across the floor, along the walls, and up to the ceiling in an attempt to surround their prey.

Bobby screamed, piercing and shrill.

Santa squeezed the trigger lever, spraying the room with a steady stream of fire.

The first advance of alien creatures shrieked as they burst into flames. Fireballs of slashing tentacles dropped from the ceiling and walls. They ricocheted across the floor like flaming pin balls. Walls, floor, and ceiling were blackened and charred. The stench of thick smoke and burnt flesh choked the air.

Soon the pain-riddled shrieks died. The burning creatures finally lay still, littering the battlefield that once was Bobby's room. But behind that first failed advance came a second swarm of creatures. Shrieks again filled the room but this time ringing with rage rather than as a response to pain.

Again, Bobby screamed.

Santa squeezed the flamethrower's trigger lever. But this time no fire shot forth. Even the small flame at the gun's nozzle extinguished itself. The old man had made a fatal error. No fuel remained in the tanks.

Santa and Bobby were now surrounded.

The aliens skittered across the floor, along the walls, and overhead on the ceiling. They advanced on their prey, screeching, jaws snapping, tentacles reaching.

This time Bobby and Santa both screamed.

GAME OVER!
YOU LOSE!

Santa dropped the game controller and moaned. "Not again."

Gideon burst through the door. "Santa, we're burning the Eve," he chimed. "The team's hitched and ready—" The elf cut his words short and groaned. "Are you still playing that video game?"

Santa shot the elf a disgusted look. "Blame yourself," he said, "you created the stupid thing. Now I'm addicted."

"You've played it about a hundred times," Gideon said. "Have you won even once?"

A defensive look crept across Santa's face. "I made it all the way to the flamethrower again."

Gideon crossed his arms. "Uh-huh," he said, tapping his small foot. "And you forgot to click on the pressure regulator at the back of the tanks again, didn't you? Used up all your fuel in one giant blaze of glory, right?"

Santa's face turned red. He muttered under his breath.

"I suppose that I died again?" Gideon asked, rolling his eyes.

Santa muttered again, fingering the controller.

"You never use me in the game to help you," the elf lectured, "or Bobby either for that matter."

"Just give me one more chance," Santa insisted. "I know I can beat it this time."

Gideon shook his head and laughed.

Outside, the wind howled. The small house shook and groaned. Windows rattled, fighting against the brute force. One double-framed window lost the battle. It flew open, smashing against both sides of the inside wall. The wind charged through the opening. With it came a crumpled piece of paper.

Santa rushed to the paper. Broken glass crunched underfoot. His white hair and beard whipped into tangled messes. He picked up the paper amongst the shards of glass and smoothed it out. He began reading. The letter set his hands to trembling and his heart to thudding.

"No," Santa whispered, "it can't be."

Fred Wiehe

.

Ghosts, Inc.

Outside, a starless, moonless night pressed down upon the small, cottage-style house. A late-October drizzle tapped against the windows. Wind shook a nearby tree, the branches scratching at the outside wall.

Inside, Tyler Godwin's bedroom was swathed in dark, ominous shadows; only his Incredible Hulk nightlight cast an eerie-green glow across the room.

The ten-year-old boy huddled under his covers in a tight ball of knotted muscles. His eyes were clamped shut, but he wasn't asleep. Sleep wouldn't come easily to him this night. In fact, there hadn't been a night when sleep had come easily to him. Not since moving into this house, anyway.

Sometimes, he thought he'd never sleep again. Chronic insomnia is what Wikipedia called it; he had looked it up. The Web site had defined the sleeping disorder as difficulty falling asleep, often associated with anxiety disorders. And besides sleeplessness, the effects could also include mental fatigue and hallucinations.

He worried about that part—the hallucinations. He had looked that up too; it meant seeing and hearing things that weren't really there. And it was seeing and hearing things—strange noises and

85

unexplained movement—that kept him up and restless at night.

But it wasn't just that. He felt things too. A freezing coldness would take over the room and seep into his bones, like when he stood in his grandpa's walk-in freezer.

And those were just the warning signs of the horrors that would ultimately follow: whispering voices, moving shadows, floating clothes, rattling picture frames, toys hurled across the room and smashing into walls.

Under the covers, Tyler shivered. Gooseflesh scurried along his skin and scalp like an army of ants. His pajamas clung to his body, damp with sweat.

He tried not to think about the frightening experiences. He prayed that another wouldn't happen tonight.

Because if anything did happen tonight, he couldn't depend on his mom for help; his mom didn't believe him. Mostly, he guessed, because nothing ever happened in any other part of the house other than his room. That and because she hadn't ever seen, heard, or felt anything herself. At first, his mom reacted quickly to the noises and the screams coming from his room; she'd run to see what was the matter. But by the time she got there it would all be over. All she would see was the scattered clothing, broken toys, shattered glass, and her hysterical son. Later, after so many sleepless nights, after so many outbursts, after so many calls for help, his mom's concern turned to annoyance, and she started reacting much slower. Not only that but she started blaming the mess and the noise on him.

She'd always say he had too much of an imagination and—

How'd she put it?

Oh yeah—a penchant for mischief, whatever that meant.

All Tyler really knew was that it meant most nights his mom stopped coming to check on him altogether. And she wouldn't let him change rooms either, no matter how much he fussed, complained, or whined. She just didn't believe him, and she started punishing him for the mess, the noise, and what she called his bad behavior.

Not being able to depend on his mom and because his father wasn't around anymore, there was nowhere to turn. There was no one to help.

And just the thought of it all happening again tonight made him want to barf, for each time the hallucinations—if that's what they were—got worse, stronger, more frightening.

He felt like crying over his helpless situation but choked back the sobs; he was ten, much too old for tears. Still, he couldn't stop his body from quaking and sweating. He couldn't stop the goose bumps from attacking his skin or the hairs on the back of his neck from standing on end. And he certainly couldn't stop the insomnia; he couldn't force himself to sleep no matter how hard he scrunched his eyes closed.

Not with the threat of another nightly visit hanging over his head.

Involuntarily, like animal instinct, Tyler's thumb found its way into his mouth. As soon as he realized what he'd done, he pulled it out, embarrassed by his babyish behavior even though no one else was there.

Instead, he put his hand between his legs and held his crotch because now suddenly he had to pee— bad. There was no way he was getting up and going to the bathroom, though. No, he was determined to hold it.

The closet door creaked.

Tyler gasped, and a tiny amount of pee leaked out. He knew the closet door was closed when he'd gotten in bed. He had checked it. Someone or something was now opening it. And he was sure that it was from the inside.

It was starting.

"Please go away," Tyler whispered. He choked back tears and squeezed his crotch harder to hold off the impending flood. "Leave me alone. Please go away."

The closet door creaked again. The answer to Tyler's pleas was *no*; whatever was in the closet was not going away.

Cold shivers slinked like slugs up Tyler's back. His heart pounded. Tears burst from his eyes, no longer able to stop himself from crying. But somehow he managed to hold the pee at bay.

Then someone or something touched him, gripping his arm in a tight grasp.

Tyler screamed. The floodgates opened. Pee streamed forth, soaking pajamas and bedding.

Something still clutched at his arm, hurting him.

Tyler squirmed and kicked. Somehow, he broke free from whatever it was that had a hold of him. He threw off the covers and sat up with a jerk.

Breathing hard, frosty plumes blew out in front of him; the air was frigid. His heart raced like a rat on an exercise wheel. Whatever it was that had grabbed him, though, was nowhere in sight.

But the closet door stood mysteriously open, just as he suspected. And the boy stared wild-eyed at the eerie, blue light emanating from within. Arcs of blue electrical currents zapped the air all around the closet doorway. They crackled and hissed, and Tyler's hair stood straight up like when he rubbed at it with a balloon.

He'd seen a lot of weird stuff before in this room, but he'd never seen anything like this.

Jumping out of bed, Tyler ran for his bedroom door. He grabbed the doorknob, turned it, and yanked as hard as he could. Even though there was no lock, the door wouldn't budge. Pounding on the door with his fists, Tyler yelled, "Mom!"

Something cold touched the back of his neck. Gasping, he whirled around. What he saw made him want to scream. In fact, he opened his mouth as if to scream but no sound came forth. Instead, all he could do was press his back against the door and watch in horror.

A ghostly, blue specter floated out of the closet. It glided across the room, never touching the ground. Blue currents of electricity sputtered and flashed like tiny lightning bolts all around it.

The air continued to crackle and hiss. Tyler's hair still stood on end. He breathed hard, breath still visible with each exhalation. Static shocks bombarded his skin as the specter got closer and closer.

When the bluish thing reached out and grabbed him, Tyler finally found his voice.

He screamed—loud and shrill.

◆◆◆

89

Tyler's mom startled awake, breath lodged in her throat like a chunk of partially chewed meat. Her son's wails shot down the hallway and slammed against her closed door.

"Not again," Aileen muttered, dislodging her held breath.

She sat up, rubbed at her sleepy eyes, and debated on whether or not to investigate yet another false cry for help.

"Why is he doing this?"

She felt like crying. What was she going to do? Ever since the divorce, ever since moving to a new house in a new town, Tyler had been acting out with these inexplicable night terrors. She knew the boy missed his father. She also knew that Tyler blamed her for the break up, probably because she had been the one to move out, taking the boy and upsetting his world. But she hoped for a fresh start...for both of them. She hoped her son's depression and anger would pass. She never imagined Tyler's emotional instability could possibly manifest itself in such an awful and horrendous way. Not for the first time she considered that her son might need therapy. Maybe they both did.

Tyler's high-pitched scream almost shook the bedroom door from its hinges.

Aileen threw back her covers and bolted out of bed. In all the nights since these night terrors started, she'd never heard a more desperate cry for help. The sound of it frayed her nerves and sent chills shuddering through her entire body. Although she suspected it was yet another false cry for help, a manipulation to punish her for whatever Tyler perceived as her fault, she could no longer just ignore it. She had to find out.

She grabbed her robe, wrapping it around her for protection against October's damp chill. She opened the bedroom door and raced down the hallway to Tyler's room. Nearing the door, her skin began to prickle. The hairs on her arms stood on end. The air crackled, hissed, and popped with static electricity.

Tyler's screams rose to fevered pitch.

And his mom was no longer so sure of her convictions. Maybe this time it wasn't just a ploy to see if she'd come running, a test to see if she really loved her son or not. Maybe this time Tyler was in real trouble—trouble of his own making surely, but still trouble. What the boy could've done to cause the bizarre electrical energy that now seemed to surge through the hallway she couldn't even imagine. But whatever he had done, it apparently had gotten out of control.

An electrical shock greeted Aileen as she grabbed and twisted the doorknob. She cried out as an energy surge burned her hand. That same energy threw her backwards across the hallway. She crashed into the wall, the impact making a sickening thud. She slid down the wall into a sitting position, groaning with misery—hand burned, back aching, head throbbing. She tried to clear the cobwebs away and get her bearings, but her vision blurred and the hallway spun.

From inside the bedroom, Tyler screamed and wailed for help.

The sound of her son's woeful cries brought Aileen's mind back to task. Soon her vision cleared, and the hallway—although it didn't stop spinning altogether—at least slowed. Slowly, she picked herself up and leaned back against the wall for support.

Tyler's bedroom door stood slightly ajar; apparently she had managed to open it before being struck down. To Aileen's horror, a bluish light radiated through the crack in the doorway, and Tyler now keened and screeched like a suffering animal.

"Tyler!" Aileen cried.

She lunged across the hallway, slamming her shoulder into the door, and bolting across the threshold. But once inside, the sheer insanity of what she experienced brought her up short: Her panted breath blew out in frosty plumes. Her skin prickled as if with a thousand pinpoints. Her hair stood straight up. All around her, luminous discharges of electricity crackled and hissed. The source of these electrical currents was some sort of blue energy field that hovered in the middle of the room. It looked suspiciously human in shape but was much larger than any person and had no facial features, no resemblance to humanity whatsoever.

Worse of all, Tyler was caught within this bizarre blue light. It somehow held the boy in midair.

"Tyler!" Aileen cried.

Tyler's eyes bugged out. His hair stood straight out in all directions. He flailed his arms and kicked his legs as if fighting to free himself but to no avail. When he heard and saw his mother, Tyler reached out and wailed, "Mommy!"

Aileen screamed, "Tyler!" She burst into tears, unsure of what she could do to save her son.

Then she realized that both Tyler and the blue light were moving away from her, back toward the closet.

"Tyler!"

She ran only two steps forward before a bolt of electricity reached out from the blue energy field and slammed into her chest. She convulsed with electric shock, dropping to her knees. From there, with tremors attacking every inch of her body, she helplessly watched the blue light take her son into the closet.

Still flailing and kicking, Tyler screamed, "Mommy!"

The closet door slammed shut.

Everything went quiet except for the patter of rain on the window and the scratching of tree branches on the outside wall. The once frigid air turned normal, and Aileen's hair no longer stood on end either.

Her body, however, still quivered uncontrollably as she dropped onto her hands and crawled like a baby across the floor. At the closet door, she reached for the knob, turned it, and pulled. The door opened easily. She collapsed to the floor in front of the open closet, twitching and trembling. Tears soaked her face. Sobs choked her throat.

The blue energy field had vanished. Tyler was gone.

◆◆◆

Outside, darkness held an oncoming dawn at bay. Rain tapped on every window like an unwelcome caller trying to wake the people within. The five people inside, however, were not asleep and hadn't slept all night. Instead, they gathered in the living room, at a small, round table, preparing for a séance.

Three white votive candles flickered within glass holders on the round table. Except for the glowing screens of two laptop computers positioned nearby on a foldout table, the candles created the only light in the dark room. Snakes of gray cables and wires slithered across the floor, connecting the laptops to other equipment positioned about the room: a video camera, a voice recorder, infrared motion detectors, an electromagnetic field detector, an ambient air thermometer, and vibration monitors.

Cree Wildwood and Patricia Weir—young college students at San Jose State and paranormal investigators for Ghosts, Inc.—sat at the round table with the two homeowners. Skyler Rumson—another student at San Jose State and Ghosts, Inc.'s bespectacled Tech Specialist—manned the computers. At his side, as always, was a can of Dr. Pepper. He slugged some down as he prepared to record and monitor everything that took place during the séance.

Cree had started Ghosts, Inc. over a year ago for the sole purpose of investigating paranormal activity and the existence of ghosts. After recruiting friends Patricia and Skyler, the three partners ran the operation from Cree's dorm room. They had their own MySpace page and posted videos of their investigations on YouTube, all in the hopes of someday getting their own cable television show like Ghost Hunters, Paranormal State, or True Hauntings.

The young homeowners, Jim and Cathy Cook, had contacted the fledgling ghost hunters to help rid their new home of what they suspected to be paranormal activity—lights turning off and on, strange noises, moving objects, and possessions missing—resulting in this séance.

Cree ran a hand through his thick, blond hair as he turned to the homeowners and whispered, "It's nearly 3am. Because Jesus died at 3pm, the exact opposite time, 3am is considered a mockery of his death. That's why most ghost hunters believe that this is when paranormal activity is supposedly at its peak."

Jim and Cathy clasped hands and nodded. Fear shadowed their expectant faces.

"You've met Patricia," Cree continued. "She's a sensitive. She'll conduct the séance, attempting to contact the spirit or spirits you say have been haunting your home."

Patricia gave the couple a nervous smile. As she hooked her long, straight hair behind one ear, she blushed a bit at the sudden expectation for her to perform.

"Do you understand?" Cree asked the couple.

Jim and Cathy looked at each other. As if they had spoken telepathically, Jim answered for both of them. "We understand."

"Good," Cree said. "So we have your permission to proceed?"

Determination crept across Cathy's face. She sat up and squared her shoulders in a brave stance, but her voice cracked with apprehension as she spoke. "We've only been married a year," she said. "This is our first house, our first real home. We've just found out that I'm pregnant; we're going to be bringing up a child here soon. We want this spirit or thing gone, out of our lives." Tears welled in her eyes.

Jim gave his wife's hand a gentle squeeze. He

said, "We just want to feel safe in our own home. You have our permission. Let's do this."

Patricia took out two Saint Michael medals on delicate silver chains. She let them dangle from her long, slender fingers. "Before we go on," she explained, "I want you two to put these on for protection." She handed the medals to Jim and Cathy.

Jim took the medals, giving one to his wife. As the two put the chains around their necks, Jim asked, "What about the rest of you?"

"We're already wearing ours," Patricia answered.

After slugging down some Dr. Pepper, Skyler said, "Sorry to interrupt." His glasses slipped down his nose. Pushing them back in place, he continued, "But it's time."

Patricia nodded. Her pretty face took on a look of grim resolve. "Let's get started," she said. She placed three protective crystals in front of her on the table: Black Tourmaline, Hematite, and Apache Tear. Afterward, she said, "Everyone except Skyler place your hands flat on the table. Spread your fingers wide. Our hands should make a circle and touch. The circle should not be broken. Everyone understand?"

Everyone nodded in agreement and did as Patricia commanded.

Once the circle of hands was complete, Patricia closed her eyes as if entering a trance. She began, "We call upon the spirit or spirits which haunt this home and trouble this couple. Come to us. Show yourselves."

The flickering candlelight danced across the

darkened room. Drizzle tapped against the windowpanes. Otherwise, nothing moved and only silence answered.

No one at the table moved either or hardly breathed, for that matter. Even Skyler at his computers remained still and quiet, studying the monitors and overseeing the equipment; he didn't even dare adjust his glasses or take a drink of Dr. Pepper.

Undaunted, Patricia continued, "You cannot deny us. I command you to come. Give us a sign that you're here."

Cathy gasped. "My God," she said, "I just felt a strange coldness on my neck. I think something touched me."

"I feel it too," Patricia confirmed, "a chill, deep in my bones. Someone or something is here with us."

"Are you getting anything on the equipment, Sky?" Cree asked.

While the group discussed the possibility of a paranormal presence, Skyler took the opportunity to sneak a drink of Dr. Pepper. Now, confronted with a direct question, he swallowed hard before answering. "No drop in temperature," he said, choking a bit. "No change in the electromagnetic field either." He adjusted his glasses and snuck another drink of soda.

"Don't break the circle," Patricia reminded everyone. "Someone or something is here with us, whether the equipment confirms it or not."

"Okay, Patricia," Cree said, "continue."

Patricia nodded. "Was that you?" she asked the air in hopes that she was right. "Did you touch

Cathy? Are you trying to reach out to us?"

Tapping drizzle answered again.

"Give us another sign," Patricia pleaded, "make a noise of some kind to prove you're here."

As if answering Patricia's pleas, all of the infrared motion detectors began to chime.

Everyone startled. Gasps and squeals escaped from just about everyone in the room. Hands covered gaping mouths or clutched at Saint Michael medals. The circle was broken. The chimes stopped.

Patricia sighed, "It's over. We broke the circle. Whatever or whoever was here is gone."

"Sky, what set off those motion detectors?" Cree asked.

Skyler shrugged. "Nothing from the vibration monitors to indicate movement of any kind, normal or paranormal," he answered, pushing his slipping glasses back in place. "I didn't see anything or anyone on the computer monitors from the video camera. As far as I know, we didn't record any unusual sounds." Skyler shrugged again. "There's no reason for those motion detectors to go off, Cree."

"The very fact that they did go off, and for no apparent reason, proves paranormal activity," Patricia insisted.

"I know I felt something touch me," Cathy agreed.

"What do we do now?" asked Jim.

Cree ran a hand through his thick hair and thought for a moment. "I'm not sure we have undeniable proof of paranormal activity," he said. "In other words, I'm not sure we have a true haunting here."

Patricia pouted. "Cree, I really think—"

Cree held up a hand to interrupt. He said, "But I think it best to side with caution. I think we should do a spiritual cleansing." Cree looked at the homeowners and said, "With your permission."

"Yes, please," Cathy pleaded.

Jim nodded in agreement.

While Skyler drank Dr. Pepper and recorded the proceedings, the other two investigators made their way throughout the house; they hung crucifixes, sprinkled Holy Water, and said prayers.

When finished, the team of Ghosts, Inc. left Cathy and Jim Cook with the two Saint Michael medals they had given the couple earlier. The ghost hunters also promised that they would return anytime if needed.

♦♦♦

In the morning, Patricia and Skyler met at Cree's dorm room. Cree was nowhere around. But since the door was unlocked, they let themselves in. As usual the small, single room was a mess, with clothes strewn about on both the unmade bed and the floor. Books were stacked everywhere and papers littered the place.

Skyler sat down at Cree's desk. He cleared it off, took out his laptop, and booted it up. Meanwhile, he hooked up headphones to the computer and put them on.

Patricia retrieved a can of Dr. Pepper from Cree's mini-refrigerator and placed it on the desk next to Skyler's laptop. Then she stood behind the Tech Specialist to watch him work.

Skyler looked up over his shoulder at the tall, slender girl. He pushed his glasses back up his nose and grinned. "Thanks," he said.

Patricia hooked dark, straight hair behind one ear. Smiling back, she said, "No problem."

Skyler popped the top on the can. He took a huge slug before going back to work.

Patricia stood very still and quiet, watching the computer screen with complete fascination.

The computer displayed a grey screen with a blue line running horizontally across the middle. The blue line sometimes jumped and skipped like on a polygraph test when someone lied. But Patricia knew that Skyler wasn't monitoring honesty. He was listening to sound recordings from last night's séance, and the line jigged and jagged according to the volume of each sound recorded. She also knew that this talented computer geek was using a program called Audacity Audio Editor to clean up background noise, such as static, hisses, or hums in the hopes of catching something they hadn't heard last night with their imperfect human ears. Mostly, he would be listening for Electronic Voice Phenomena; otherwise known in the ghost hunting business as EVP's—voices speaking from beyond the grave.

"Whoa!" Skyler exclaimed much too loud because of the headphones on his ears. He took the headphones off, turned slightly in his seat, and grinned up at Patricia. "You got to hear this," he said in a more normal volume. Unplugging his headphones, Skyler turned on the computer's speaker. "Listen." He played back the recording.

On the recording, just before the motion detectors chimed, there was what sounded like a muffled voice.

Patricia's pretty face scrunched with uncertainty. She asked, "Was that one of us?"

Skyler took a drink of Dr. Pepper, adjusted his glasses, and shook his head. "That wasn't any of us."

"Play it again."

Skyler did.

Patricia shook her head. "I still can't make that out," she said, disappointed. "Can you clean it up more?"

"I'll try." Skyler went back to work for a few minutes. Then he said, "Okay, listen now." He played the recording again.

First they heard Patricia say, "Give us another sign...make a noise of some kind to prove you're here."

Then they again heard the muffled voice. They could still hardly make it out but both now swore they heard it say, "I'm here."

Right afterward, the motion detectors chimed.

"We've got an EVP recording," Patricia exclaimed, grinning from ear to ear. "I'm positive we just heard a ghost talk to us." She bent down and gave Skyler a peck on the cheek. "You're a genius."

Skyler turned red as he adjusted his slipping glasses. He knew a girl as pretty and as popular as Patricia would never really be interested in a geek like him; Cree—blond, handsome, and athletic—was more Patricia's type. But still, the girl had never kissed him before. Maybe she liked brains over brawn? Maybe a geek stood a chance, after all?

"Is there anything you don't know, Sky?" Patricia beamed.

"Well, it's not knowledge that's important,"

101

Skyler responded modestly and took a sip of Dr. Pepper.

"Oh, it's not?" Patricia asked with arched eyebrows.

Skyler shook his head. He adjusted his glasses. "I like to consider myself imaginative more than knowledgeable. After all, Einstein said, 'Imagination is more important than knowledge. Knowledge is limited. Imagination encircles the world.' I live by that."

Patricia squeezed Skyler's shoulders with affection. She said, "Well, in my book you have both."

Just then Cree stormed into the room. He carried a newspaper in hand and a wicked grin on his face.

"Cree," Patricia squealed, "you've got to hear this. We recorded an actual EVP from last night."

Cree stepped up next to Patricia, behind Skyler. "Let me hear it."

Skyler played the recording.

A strained look crept across Cree's face. "I don't hear it," he said.

Skyler played it again.

"Nope, sorry, still don't," Cree insisted. He gave a dismissive shrug and said, "Upload it onto both our MySpace page and to YouTube." Turning away, he plopped onto his messy bed.

Patricia squeezed Skyler's shoulders again and bent close. "I heard it," she whispered, "and it's hecka exciting."

Sitting on his bed, Cree spread out the newspaper. "Listen up, you guys. Something phenomenal happened last night."

Skyler remained at the computer, uploading the

files. Patricia plopped down next to Cree on the bed.

"According to the paper," Cree continued, "a woman was arrested last night on suspicion of murdering her ten-year-old son."

"Yuck!" Patricia said.

Skyler swiveled his chair around to face Cree and Patricia. "What's that got to do with us?" he asked, reaching back for the can of Dr. Pepper.

"Yeah, we don't do murders, Cree," Patricia insisted.

"Give a guy a chance," Cree pleaded.

Patricia and Skyler both shrugged, giving Cree nonverbal cues to continue.

"First, no body was found," Cree said, "and no blood, either. Second, the only sign of any foul play was the messy state of the boy's bedroom."

Skyler pushed up his glasses and looked around. "If messy bedrooms were a crime, you'd be in San Quentin, bro."

Cree beamed. "Exactly," he said.

Patricia wrinkled her nose as if at a horrible stench. "Well, what makes them think the woman killed her son then?"

"Because the woman called 911," Cree said, scanning the paper.

Skyler swallowed a slug of Dr. Pepper before asking, "So she confessed?"

Cree shook his head. "No. According to this, she claimed her son was—and I quote—'abducted into the closet by a blue electrical storm.' Do you believe it?"

Skyler finished off his Dr. Pepper. He set the can down and stood. "A blue electrical storm appeared in the kid's bedroom—inside the house—took the

103

kid and then disappeared inside the closet?"

Cree grinned.

Patricia smacked Cree on the shoulder. "Stop looking so amused. The kid is probably dead. The poor woman is obviously crazy."

"Oh, is she?" Cree asked.

Skyler moved closer. "You think she's telling the truth. You think this blue, electrical storm exists…that it's some kind of paranormal activity…maybe even a ghost."

Cree's grin widened. "I think we need to find out."

"Are *you* crazy," Patricia squealed.

"This could be our biggest case yet," Cree explained. "Think of the publicity if we can prove her story's true and that some sort of paranormal activity is responsible for the missing kid." Cree shrugged. "Heck, maybe the kid's still alive. Maybe we can save him." He looked from Patricia to Skyler. "We'd be heroes, guys. We'd be sure to get our own show."

Patricia and Skyler exchanged glances.

"This is the kind of case we've always dreamed about," Cree continued.

Skyler pushed his glasses into place. He asked, "Why isn't this front page news? You're on page twelve. Where'd this take place anyway?"

Cree scanned the paper again. "A little town north of here called Weed."

"Weed," Patricia exclaimed, "there's a town named Weed?"

Skyler sat down at his computer and did a quick search for Weed, CA. He soon found a map and the city's official Web site. "Weed is more than three hundred and fourteen miles north of here, off US-97 by Klamath Falls," he said. "It's almost to the Oregon border." Swiveling his chair back around to again face his friends, he added, "It's a five hour drive. You want to go there?"

"That's right. What else does it say?"

Skyler swiveled around and studied the information on the screen. "It's a general law city incorporated in 1961. It's a clean, safe, attractive, rural community…an unspoiled mountain environment."

"Sounds great," Cree exclaimed. "We could use a vacation." He jumped up from the bed. "Let's pack everything up. We can be there before nightfall."

"How are we going to find the exact house?" Patricia asked as she too stood. "The paper doesn't give the address."

Cree grinned. "We look for the house surrounded by yellow, crime-scene tape and a sign that tells us to keep out."

"And you think we'll just be able to walk right in, make ourselves at home, and have a little séance without anyone noticing?" Skyler asked, shaking his head with disbelief.

"Well, we'll have to be sneaky about it," Cree said, rolling his eyes at Skyler's naiveté. "Now let's rock and roll."

Patricia shot Skyler a look of pure wonderment. "He *is* crazy," she said.

Skyler shrugged. Then a look of concern crossed his face. "Hey, tomorrow's Halloween," he said, gulping hard. "By the time we do our séance it will be Halloween."

105

"Yes," Cree bellowed, "even better."

"B-But…b-b-but…"

"What's the matter, Sky, you got a hot date bobbing for apples?" Patricia asked with a sly grin and a wink. "Maybe going trick or treating?"

Skyler sighed. "Let's rock and roll," he mumbled.

◆◆◆

A beat-up VW van rolled into the quaint city of Weed, CA well after dark. A light drizzle spotted the van windows and dampened the streets. Cree drove. Patricia sat in the passenger seat. Skyler sat in back with the equipment. They had already stopped at a small grocery store on Main Street, bought some Dr. Pepper, Tostitos, and salsa, and discreetly asked about the bizarre incident and the house where it had occurred. While enthusiastically telling the story, the young grocery clerk had inadvertently told them where to find the house.

Now, the van pulled up to that small, cottage-style home. It stood well back and off the road, nestled within a clump of fir trees. An electrical tower grew up out of the backyard, a metal behemoth rising into the dark sky. Small, white lights blinked at the very top, no doubt a warning to low-flying aircraft. Power lines ran from the monstrous structure to two others, both about a hundred yards away in different directions; small white lights blinked atop those, as well. In fact— even though the metal towers themselves weren't visible in the night—white lights blinked in the sky in both directions, getting tinier and dimmer, until finally disappearing from sight altogether.

The three ghost hunters climbed out of the van.

"Perfect," Cree said. "There aren't any neighbors close enough or within direct view of the house. I'll park the van around back in case the local police do a drive by. No one will even know we're here."

"How do we get in?" Skyler asked. He took his glasses off and wiped rain off the lenses. Putting them back on, he added, "I'm sure the police have the place locked up tight."

Cree ran a hand through his wet hair. "I'll get us inside," he insisted, "don't you worry."

All three climbed back inside the van. Cree drove it around back, parked, and turned off the headlights. Outside again, Cree ripped the crime scene tape and all three stepped up onto the back porch. They ignored the sign that the police posted on the door stating that the premises was a crime scene and that no one should enter under penalty of prosecution. The police had also padlocked the door. That didn't stop them either. In his hand, Cree carried a large pair of metal cutters that took care of the padlock in swift order. It dropped like an anchor, clunking onto the porch.

"Told you I'd get us inside," Cree whispered, opening the backdoor.

"You're going to get us in the state pen too," Patricia whispered back.

"I've got claustrophobia," Skyler muttered, "I can't go to prison."

"That's not the only reason you can't go to prison, creampuff," Cree scoffed.

"Funny," Skyler replied, "very funny."

Patricia smacked them both. "Can we go inside now?"

"Okay, stop hitting." Cree rubbed his arm. "Let's start unloading the equipment."

Under the cover of night, the three ghost hunters unloaded large equipment cases. Inside, they used only flashlights with red filters fitted to the lenses to light their way. The house was small, so finding the boy's messy bedroom took little time. From the cases, they unpacked two computers, a video camera, a four-channel DVR, a full-spectrum camera, a voice recorder, motion detectors, vibration monitors, EMF detectors, ambient air thermometers, and rolls of gray cables and wires. They worked in tandem, methodically setting up the equipment, with only the red lights from their flashlights and the boy's Incredible Hulk nightlight to guide them.

Afterward, facing the boy's closed closet, they sat on the floor in the dark—flashlights turned off. While they waited, the three drank Dr. Pepper and ate Tostitos with salsa. The crunching of tortilla chips and the gulping of soda helped drown out the eerie sounds of their own rapid heartbeats that kept time with the pitter patter of raindrops on the windows and the tree branches that scratched against the wall, sounding like cats sharpening their claws.

After slugging down some Dr. Pepper, Skyler whispered, "While we were driving out here from the grocery store in town I got on the Internet and searched public records for information on this house."

"Find anything interesting?" Cree asked.

Skyler pushed his glasses back up his nose. "Actually, yeah, I did."

"What?" Patricia asked.

Skyler leaned closer as if sharing a secret and the three of them weren't the only people within earshot. He muttered, "A few years ago, before Aileen and Tyler Godwin moved to Weed, a woman and her son lived in this house. Their names were Ginny and Tommy Brewer. One night, Ginny Brewer's ex-husband Jack broke into the house. He beat up Ginny and kidnapped Tommy. Jack and Tommy Brewer were never seen again; they just disappeared. Ginny Brewer was so distraught that she committed suicide. She hanged herself right inside that closet."

Patricia gasped. She smacked Skyler on the arm. "You're making this up, Sky."

"Stop," Skyler pleaded, rubbing his arm. "Swear to God I'm not."

Cree studied the closet door with new appreciation. "You think the blue electrical storm that Aileen Godwin described is the ghost of Ginny Brewer?"

Skyler nodded. "And that she took Tyler to replace her own kidnapped son," he added.

Patricia shook her head. "But how does a ghost become a blue electrical storm?"

Skyler munched on chips. With a full mouth, he mumbled, "I chalk that up to the woman's hysteria. I doubt there really was any kind of electrical storm." He swallowed and took a drink of soda. "The shock of seeing a ghost and having her son taken could account for that wild description."

Cree nodded. "Maybe," he agreed. He took out his cell phone and checked the time. "It's almost midnight," he said, pocketing the cell.

"Halloween," Skyler hissed.

"That's right," Cree said, "and I say we don't wait until 3am to do our séance. I say we do it now."

Somewhere in the house a clock chimed twelve times, signaling the hour of midnight and the beginning of Halloween.

All three startled. Afterward, the three ghost hunters stared at each other, chuckled nervously, and tried to catch their collective breaths and calm their racing hearts.

Once calmed, Patricia said, "Okay, let's start. Get in a circle."

The three of them maneuvered on the floor to make a circle.

"Now," Patricia continued, "we place our hands on the floor in front of us, fingertips touching, making another circle with our hands."

They did as instructed.

"Wait," Cree said. "All the equipment set to record, Sky?"

"Any movement, change in temperature, or change in electromagnetic field should automatically start the video camera, the full-spectrum camera, and the sound recorder."

Cree nodded. "Good. If anything happens, I don't want to miss it. Okay, go ahead, Patricia."

Patricia closed her eyes. "Ginny Brewer, are you here with us?" she asked. "Give us a sign that you're here."

Holding their collective breaths, the ghost hunters waited.

No answer.

Patricia continued, "Ginny, did you take Tyler? Is he with you?"

No answer.

"Ginny, we're not here to hurt you. Please don't be afraid to show yourself. Come to us. We only want to help."

A creak answered. The closet door opened a crack. Chimes from the motion detectors and vibration monitors sounded a warning of the oncoming storm.

Cree and Skyler both gasped. Patricia let out a sharp squeal.

Behind his glasses, Skyler's eyes almost popped out of his head. "D-D-Do you guys…see that?"

A bright, blue light emanated through the door's opening, casting itself across the tiny bedroom and slicing it in half like a sharp knife.

"My God," Cree declared.

"Ginny, is that you?" Patricia whispered; fear cracked her voice.

As if in response, tiny lightning bolts flashed at the door's opening. The air crackled with static electricity, raising the hackles of the three ghost hunters. The temperature in the room plummeted.

Patricia shivered. All three panted hard, breath visible in the frosty air.

Skyler gulped. "I stand corrected," he whispered. "There is some kind of electrical storm in that closet. But for the life of me—"

The closet door flung open, hitting the wall with a bang. A blinding blue light shone from inside the closet. Luminous, blue arcs of electrical currents zapped the room.

"This can't be good," Skyler moaned.

The energized air crackled, hissed, and popped like frying bacon. Everyone's hair stood straight up.

"What's happening," Skyler exclaimed. "I feel

111

like I'm being tortured by a mad acupuncturist."

Patricia shushed him. "Hear that?" she asked.

"I can't hear anything but the chimes and the crazy electrical storm," Cree said.

"Listen," Patricia replied."

A tiny voice rose above the other noise. It sounded thin and faraway.

"Tyler!" Patricia cried. "Is that you, Tyler?"

All three concentrated on hearing an answer.

Chimes continued to ring. Rain tapped steadily against the windows. The tree branches scratched an itch on the outside wall. Static electricity crackled, hissed, and popped.

But unmistakably the tiny, thin voice grew in strength and volume.

"I hear it," Cree murmured. "But what's it saying? I can't make it out."

"Me either," Skyler agreed.

Patricia called out to the boy again. "Tyler, where are you? We're looking for you! We're here to help!"

With those declarations, the electromagnetic energy in the room spiked. The power from the blue storm slithered and hissed through the room like thousands of snakes. Thunder rumbled all around. The motion and vibration detectors resonated louder, faster, sounding panicked. The small house shook as if in the throes of a powerful earthquake.

"Whoa!" Skyler howled. "I'm about ready to jump out of my skin."

"Don't break the circle," Patricia warned. "We'll lose contact with the boy."

A large, blue specter drifted out of the closet and across the room. All around it blue lightning bolts sputtered and flashed. It reached out with an arcing discharge of energy that surrounded the three ghost hunters, lifting them into the air and spinning them in different directions.

Patricia screamed. Skyler wailed. Cree yowled. The shrill of their collective cries rang over the chimes and supernatural noises echoing throughout the room.

The circle was broken but didn't seem to matter. Rather than disappearing, the specter grew in size and power. Like a child throwing toys during a tantrum, it tossed each ghost hunter in opposite directions across the room. Each of them crashed into a different wall and dropped to the floor—*thud, thud, thud.*

No one moved or made a sound; consciousness had been stolen from all three victims.

With that, the specter retreated into the closet. The door slammed shut. The electrical storm inside the room died. The house stood still.

◆◆◆

When the ghost hunters regained consciousness all was deadly quiet. The only sounds in the room were the collective groans and moans of Cree, Patricia, and Skyler as they picked themselves up off the floor. Each checked for broken or fractured bones. Fortunately, no one had more than a few scrapes and bruises, sore muscles, and a bloody nose or mouth.

Cree straightened. He limped to Patricia. "You okay?" he asked.

Patricia rubbed at sore muscles and stretched. "I think so," she answered while running her fingers like a comb through her hair. She eyed Cree. "Your

113

nose is bleeding."

Cree dabbed at his nose with his shirt sleeve. "I'll be alright," he said.

Patricia looked over at Skyler who was picking through the rubble for his glasses and placing them back onto his face; one of the lenses was cracked. "What about you, Sky?"

Skyler hobbled over to them. He was wiping blood from the corner of his mouth. "Physically just a few bumps and bruises," he said, "but emotionally scarred for life. Let's get out of here."

"Not so fast," Cree said, running a hand through his thick hair. "What exactly happened? Anybody got any ideas?"

"I have some theories," Skyler said, "none good." He stared at the closet door. "Let's get out," he repeated.

Cree rubbed at the back of his aching neck. "I don't know," he said, "maybe we *should* bail while we can. Pack up the equipment and get out."

"No," Patricia squealed. "We can't leave Tyler to that…that…thing."

"We don't even know if that was Tyler we heard or not," Cree said.

Skyler no longer stared at the closet door. He now drank in Patricia's face, her pretty features crinkled with worry and alarm. Sighing, resigned to knowing he couldn't bail no matter how frightened, not as long as Patricia wanted to stay, he said, "Let me check my equipment. Maybe we recorded something that could help us decide."

Skyler sat down in front of a laptop and the voice recorder. Putting on headphones, he went to work cleaning up whatever the recorder had captured during the séance.

Patricia and Cree joined him, standing behind and watching over his shoulder.

Soon Skyler took the headphones off. He turned and looked back over his shoulder at his two cohorts. "Listen to this," he said.

From the recorder—right after Patricia called out to Tyler—a boy's thin, frightened voice said, "Help me."

"Did you hear it?" Skyler asked.

Both Cree and Patricia nodded.

"He's here," Patricia insisted, "being held in that closet."

Cree turned and looked at the closet door. He strode to it with determination.

"Cree," Patricia cried. "Don't."

But Cree didn't listen. He grabbed the doorknob and yanked hard. The door opened easily. There was nothing inside except clothes, shoes, and toys. "Being held where?" Cree asked, dumbfounded.

Patricia thought for a moment before venturing a guess. She said, "Somewhere between two worlds…somewhere between life and death."

"Great," Skyler lamented.

"Okay, say you're right," Cree said. "How do we get him back? How do we exorcize this ghost, if that's what it is?" He turned to Skyler. "Sky, you said you had a theory or two, didn't you?"

Skyler sighed. He muttered, "Yeah, stupidly I said that." Turning back to his computer, he checked readings taken during the séance. Afterward, he swiveled in his chair, stood, and joined his friends at the closet. He said, "I just checked the readings taken on the electromagnetic field during the séance.

115

It spiked like nothing I've ever seen before."

"There was a lot of power being channeled through here, that's for sure," Cree agreed. "How's that help us?"

"I think it explains why Ginny Brewer's ghost has become what it has…become."

"What do you mean?" Patricia urged.

Skyler adjusted his broken glasses. He took a deep, calming breath. "Spirits not only give off electromagnetic energy," he said, "but they feed off existing EM fields too."

"What's your point?" Cree asked.

"The Earth is one huge magnetic field," Skyler explained. "It's naturally in the atmosphere and in all life, acting like a force field, carrying energy, and capable of producing action. Add electrical devices, computers, cell phones, and other man-made devices…and you just increased the natural EMF."

"I think I know where you're going with this," Patricia said. She moved to a window and stared out at the blinking lights atop the mammoth electrical tower. "Ginny Brewer isn't just creating her own EM field or feeding off the natural EM field or even feeding off the usual man-made devices. She's draining huge amounts of energy from those power lines."

Skyler nodded. "That's why she's manifesting in such a powerful way, like nothing we've ever seen or heard of before."

Cree joined Patricia at the window. He too stared at the blinking lights atop the tower. "The overdose of energy has made her a monster," he hissed.

"That's right," Skyler confirmed. "That energy

116

combined with anger and confusion has made her entity fierce and brutal. She's not going to give Tyler up without a fight."

Cree wheeled on the Tech Specialist. "So what do we do? I don't think a usual cleansing is going to do the trick."

"No, I doubt it," Skyler agreed. "That's why we should get out now." He looked at Patricia.

Patricia shook her head. "No," she said, "we're not leaving Tyler." She studied Skyler's face, squinting as if reading fine print. "You're holding back," she finally said. "I know you; you've got an idea."

Skyler adjusted his glasses. He shifted uneasily from foot to foot. "It's crazy," he said. "It'll probably never work."

"Wouldn't Einstein say that anything was possible?" Patricia asked. "Doesn't imagination encircle the world?"

"Me and my big mouth," Skyler scolded himself. "Okay," he continued. "Ever hear of an Electromagnetic Pulse Bomb?" he asked.

"Yeah, in science fiction," Cree snorted. "You're right; it's crazy. You might as well be talking cyborgs from the future, man."

Skyler shook his head. "Not so much science fiction anymore," he said.

"I'd listen to him, Cree," Patricia said. "He's a geek genius when it comes to these things."

Skyler blushed. "Thanks," he said. Despite his growing fear, he now grinned from ear to ear.

Cree said, "Okay, geek genius, explain it to us. But in plain English so stupid people like us can understand."

"Hey, speak for yourself," Patricia said, half laughing.

"Governments have been working on the theory that a high-altitude nuclear blast can create an electromagnetic shock wave that can in effect irreversibly fry all electronic equipment within a very wide radius, leaving their enemies powerless and defenseless." Skyler paused to let that information sink in. After a moment, he continued, "Smaller E-Bombs, placed within the vicinity of the equipment you want to fry can do the same on a smaller scale, kind of like a lightning strike. You can actually buy high-power microwave bombs on the Russian black market for about $150,000. The Russians call them "beer cans."

"That's all well and good," Cree responded, "but we don't have $150,000. And even if we did, we can't just call up the Russian Mafia."

"You're right," Skyler agreed. He took a deep breath. "But I might be able to build a small one."

"Build an E-Bomb," Cree scoffed, "you?"

Skyler gave Cree a hurt look. He said, "Yeah, me!"

"Wait a minute, guys," Patricia said, "we're not blowing up the place, are we? I don't see how that's going to help get Tyler back."

Skyler shook his head. "Relax, Patricia. An E-Bomb won't harm us, the house, or the town. It'll only fry anything putting out an EM field. That's the beauty…war without destruction. You bring down your enemy's power grid and virtually leave them defenseless."

"So Ginny Brewer won't have all that massive energy in which to feed off?" Cree asked.

118

"That's right," Skyler confirmed, "diminishing her power and turning her back into an ordinary, everyday spirit." Skyler paused. "At least in theory," he added.

"So if this E-Bomb works then we're hoping to help Ginny crossover with a cleansing ritual?" Cree asked.

"And save Tyler?" Patricia added. "Bring him back to this world?"

"That's the plan," Skyler confirmed. He paused and then continued, "Just one problem, though."

Cree laughed but without humor. "Just one?" he asked.

Skyler shrugged. He said, "I plan on making a Radio Frequency Weapon by using our cell phones. The RF radiation in the antennas should do the job and create an intense pulse of RF energy. And just to be sure we have enough power I'll strip apart EMF meters and mix those into the components too." Skyler thought for a moment. Then, he asked, "Patricia, do you have any Lodestones?"

"Of course," Patricia answered. "You know I always keep crystals and minerals handy."

Cree looked puzzled. He asked, "Lodestones?"

Patricia nodded. "Magnetite," she answered, "magnetized iron oxide."

Cree still looked puzzled.

Now Patricia sighed. "Lodestones have very magical properties. They should definitely add to the force of taking out the EM field and disrupting all power."

Cree shrugged. "I'm still not sure I fully comprehend but that doesn't really matter. I trust you guys." Then he looked at Skyler. "So, okay,

119

what's the problem then?"

"I can create the E-Bomb, no problem," Skyler answered. "And we can strip down some of this equipment, as well. Bare wires and exposed components will accelerate the process like throwing gas on a fire," the Tech Specialist explained. "But I need a detonator…something to set the E-Bomb off. Obviously, we don't have a nuclear device. We also don't have an explosive propellant driven generator or a high-power microwave source, which are the usual theoretical ways of detonation." He shrugged. "Sorry, but I can't think of a way to set the thing off."

Cree thought for a moment. Then a big grin spread across his face. "You're not the only genius," he said.

Patricia arched her eyebrows. "Really," she said, "enlighten us."

"Skyler already explained that the ghost of Ginny Brewer is both drawing on the energy field around her and creating energy herself," Cree answered. "We already know that the EM field really spiked when the specter appeared, especially since we apparently made it mad by trying to communicate with Tyler." He paused for effect then said, "So the specter itself will detonate the E-Bomb."

"Huh?" Skyler said.

"We throw the E-Bomb right into the middle of all that supernatural energy while the specter is discharging high-powered electrical currents," Cree continued.

Skyler nodded with approval. "I think that would do it," he agreed.

"So I'm a genius?"

Skyler shook his head and grinned. "Okay…okay, you're a genius."

"Are we having another séance?" Patricia asked.

Cree nodded. He pulled out his cell phone and checked the time. "That's right," he said. "It'll be 3am in about thirty minutes. That's when we call that big, blue specter back out and really get it mad. We need that EM field to really spike."

"I better get busy," Skyler said. Then he mumbled, "I hope this works."

Patricia sighed. "I hope this helps get Tyler back."

◆◆◆

Cree and Patricia ripped open all of their electronic equipment, gutting components, and stripping wires. They also stripped bare the gray cables. Cree even smashed holes with a hammer into the bedroom walls, yanked out wires, and stripped those too. When they were finished, the torn apart components and stripped down wires and cables were scattered across the floor like the dead on a battlefield.

Meanwhile, Skyler had torn apart and gutted their three cell phones and four EMF meters. He placed the RF antennas and the components and wires, as well as three Lodestones provided by Patricia into a Dr. Pepper can in which he had cut off the top. He was sealing the can back up with duct tape just as Cree and Patricia rejoined him.

Cree shook his head. "A Dr. Pepper can? Is that the best you could do?"

Skyler peered up at Cree. "The Russians have 'beer can' E-Bombs. I have Dr. Pepper."

121

Cree laughed. "They don't really use beer cans, do they?"

"No," Skyler admitted. "They just call them that." He shrugged. "But still, it somehow seems…appropriate." He shrugged. "Besides, I don't like beer—makes me goofy."

Cree laughed. "Yeah, like you're not already."

Somewhere in the house, a clock chimed three times.

"It's 3am," Cree said. "Does everybody know what to do?"

Patricia and Skyler nodded.

Cree said, "Let's rock and roll."

◆◆◆

Cree and Patricia stood opposite the closet door. They held hands. In their other hands, Cree held a bottle of Holy Water while Patricia held a Saint Benedict Cross on a cord. Skyler stood well behind them, hidden in the shadows, clutching the makeshift E-Bomb.

Patricia gulped, throat dry. "Can we do this?" she asked. "Are we good enough?"

Cree took a deep breath. "We have to be. We don't have a choice."

Patricia nodded. "You're right. Tyler's depending on us."

Everyone was silent for a moment, listening intently for any sign of the blue specter appearing without being called forth.

Outside, the rain had stopped, and the breeze had died, so the tree no longer scratched the wall.

Dead quiet prevailed inside. Darkness engulfed the room.

Cree squeezed Patricia's sweaty hand. He could

feel the girl trembling with anticipation and fear. Then he realized that he was trembling, as well. And his mouth had gone dry, throat constricting. Gulping hard, he said, "Let's do this."

Screwing up her courage, Patricia called out not to Ginny Brewer but to the boy. "Tyler," she cried, "where are you?"

Silence answered.

"Can you hear me, Tyler?" Patricia continued. "Can you answer?"

The shrill cry of what sounded like a tortured animal answered.

"Tyler!" Patricia screamed.

The room went suddenly frigid. Plumes of frosty breath escaped from everyone's mouths. The air crackled, hissed, and popped as static electricity crawled across their skin and stood their hair on end.

"She's coming," Skyler warned.

The closet door flung open. The door slammed against the inside wall. Blinding, blue light oozed through the doorway and out into the room. Tiny lightning bolts sputtered at the edges and zapped the surrounding darkness.

Tyler's piercing shriek again shattered everyone's nerves.

"Tyler, where are you?" Patricia screamed.

The blue specter drifted out of the closet. Its glowing form was about the size of a normal woman—much smaller than when it had appeared during the first séance. Tiny lightning bolts sputtered periodically around it as it hovered just outside the doorway.

Held prisoner within its center was the boy. He dangled in midair as if seized by invisible arms.

Frantic and wide-eyed, the boy flailed his arms and kicked his legs. "Help me," he wailed; his voice high-pitched with hysteria.

From behind Cree and Patricia, Skyler yelled, "She's not giving off enough power to detonate the E-Bomb. We need her in her full glory. You've got to make her mad."

Still clasping hands, Cree and Patricia braced themselves.

"Give us the boy," Cree bellowed. "He's not your son. You have no right to him."

At that declaration, the specter doubled in size and turned an intense blue. The tiny lightning bolts transformed into arcing currents of blue, electrical discharge—crackling, hissing, popping.

"That's it," Skyler hollered. "Keep it up."

Meanwhile, Tyler's shriek intensified too, and he continued to struggle against his invisible restraints.

"We want the boy," Patricia declared. "You can't have him. He's not your son. Give him to us."

In answer, the specter grew larger, brighter, a blinding energy that everyone had to shield their eyes against. Discharging electrical currents reached out in all directions like the tentacles of an octopus. The sound of them was almost deafening. Then a boom rumbled through the room. The house shook on its foundation.

Everyone struggled to keep their feet as they protected their eyes against the specter that seemed about to go supernova.

Cree shouted, "Sky, now."

Sky shouted back, "I can't see."

"Just throw it," both Cree and Patricia screamed

simultaneously.

Skyler stepped forward to throw the E-Bomb, but he struggled to remain upright and had to turn his face away from the blinding specter.

Another thunder-like boom rumbled. A tremor quaked through the house—a massive shock wave of supernatural force.

Somehow, magically, Cree and Patricia kept their feet and remained holding hands.

Skyler, though, lost his footing just before he could throw the E-Bomb. He fell to his hands and knees. The can slipped from his grasp.

"Skyler," Cree hollered, "better hurry."

The soda can rolled across the trembling floor. Skyler crawled after it like a baby in hot pursuit of a much-wanted toy. He lunged at the can and grabbed it just before it rolled away. After struggling to his knees, he launched the E-Bomb directly into the blinding light.

Right after, Cree and Patricia released hands. Cree threw the bottle of Holy Water and Patricia threw the Saint Benedict Cross on a cord after the E-Bomb.

With that, the house rocked. Electrical discharges zapped the air and walls. Sparks flew. Light bulbs in the overhead light burst and shattered. A blinding flashpoint ignited the air. Seconds later, the specter imploded.

Thrown into darkness, the house stood still and quiet. But the air still felt unnaturally cold. No one moved or hardly breathed.

Then a vortex of white light opened within the closet. In the glow of the light, the ghost hunters could now see the spirit of Ginny Brewer. She sat on

125

the floor, weeping, with the rope she had used to hang herself still around her neck. But the Saint Benedict Cross hung there too.

And in Ginny's lap lay Tyler, unconscious and still.

Skyler struggled to his feet, joining Patricia and Cree. Patricia took Skyler's hand in hers as the three stared in awe at both Ginny and the white light that beckoned the ghost.

But Tyler still hadn't shown any sign of life and that worried them.

Without warning, Cree stepped forward. He hunkered down next to Ginny and the boy. "It's time," he told the crying ghost. "Please give me the boy."

Ginny choked back sobs. She gazed down on Tyler and gently stroked the boy's hair.

"I'll take good care of him," Cree said. He reached down and gently lifted Tyler into his arms. He smiled at Ginny and said, "I promise."

Ginny smiled back and wiped away tears.

Cree stood and carried the boy back to where Patricia and Skyler waited. He looked at Ginny and again said, "It's time."

Ginny stood effortlessly. Her feet never touched the ground. She looked at the boy in Cree's arms one last time before she turned and entered the vortex. After the ghost disappeared into the light, the vortex closed; the room again plummeted into darkness.

"Is he alive?" Patricia whispered.

In response, Tyler moaned and stirred.

"Give him to me," Patricia said. Letting go of Skyler's hand, she reached for the boy and took him into her arms.

"Let's get out of here," Skyler suggested not for the first time.

Cree laughed and led the way through the dark house.

Outside, they stood and looked into the black sky. The lights on the towers no longer blinked.

"You know," Skyler said, "we probably took out the city's entire electrical grid...heck...maybe even the grid for the entire county."

"What's worse is we fried all of our equipment and lost all evidence of any paranormal activity," Cree said.

"But we have Tyler," Patricia said.

"Thank God for that," Cree said. "But who's going to believe where and how we found him?"

Tyler moaned again. Suddenly, he wiggled in Patricia's arms and startled awake. "Help me," he shrieked and tried to break free.

Patricia held tight. "It's okay, Tyler," she said in a soothing voice, "you're safe now."

Tyler stopped struggling. When he looked at Patricia, the fear went out of his eyes. Then he fiercely hugged the girl. Sobbing, he said, "I want my mom."

Patricia hugged the boy back with the same fierce intensity. "And we're going to take you to her," she promised.

"Maybe we did lose all proof of ghostly activity and maybe we'll never get our own show," Skyler said. "But this was totally worth it. We proved to ourselves that paranormal activity actually exists. We saved Tyler. His mother will surely be released from jail. We helped a lost soul crossover. And best of all, we lived through it."

Patricia leaned over and kissed Skyler on the cheek.

Cree slapped the Tech Specialist on the back. "Happy Halloween," he said.

Skyler adjusted his glasses and grinned. "That's right," he said. "Let's go bob for apples."

"Or maybe go trick or treating," Cree added.

Patricia laughed. "We need costumes," she said, "but no ghosts...*please.*"

Now everyone laughed.

After climbing into the beat-up van, the ghost hunters drove into Weed to reunite mother and son.

Run, Run Rudy:
A Zombie's Not Too Far Behind

The dead were everywhere, snarling and growling like crazed animals too long starved. Human scent had sent them into this hunting frenzy. Now they bore down on their prey, eager for the kill, hungry for the taste of flesh and blood.

Three young fools tore through the streets with desperate purpose. Like an NFL fullback, Brian led the way, rumbling a step or two ahead of the others, right hand firmly around the old 9mm Baretta he had brought along for protection. Rudy clutched Theresa's hand, pulling his petite girlfriend along as best he could, she barely able to keep up with his longer strides, staggering and tripping behind him but holding firm to his sweaty, freckled hand. In Rudy's other hand he clutched a small Christmas tree, brown and dry, most of its needles scattering on the breeze and pelting the oncoming zombie pack chasing them.

Fred Wiehe

Stupidly, they had left the safety of the underground compound for nothing more than a half-dead tree to help celebrate a long-forgotten holiday. What had they been thinking? Rudy had known better. But Theresa had insisted, begged, and pleaded. It had been three years since this retched infection had overtaken the city and sent the survivors underground. With no tree the last two years and this year almost everyone acting like Scrooge, she had desperately wanted something to give people hope, to bring back the Christmas spirit. Remembering a small pine tree in her old neighbor's yard, the three of them had recklessly set out to cut it down. Rudy understood why he had gone along— he loved the pretty, little blonde with the idiotic plan. But he couldn't figure out why Brian had agreed to it.

The three of them zigzagged through a maze of old, abandoned cars and knocked over anything in their path to desperately slow their pursuers. But they were still several blocks from safety, and the pack not only kept hot on their trail but had gained some ground.

"Shoot them," Rudy screamed at Brian. "They're gaining…shoot them."

But Brian didn't respond, didn't turn around, didn't even slow his pace. Maybe he hadn't heard Rudy's pleading. Maybe he didn't stop and shoot because Rudy and Theresa were in his direct line of fire. Maybe he didn't think he could get a shot off in time. Maybe blind fear possessed and controlled his every thought and action.

"Shoot them," Rudy screamed again.

"This way," Brian yelled back. The big guy

130

turned sharply down a narrow alleyway, tall buildings on both sides.

Rudy and Theresa stopped cold, she gasping for air, he yelling, "That's not the way."

Theresa screamed, "They're coming."

"Not down there," Rudy called to Brian, "it's a dead end."

Theresa pulled Rudy away from the ally. "We've got to go."

"What's he doing?" Rudy shook the tree in exasperation, brown needles flying off like hundreds of exclamation marks. "What's he thinking?"

"We've got to go," Theresa screamed again, pulling on him with all her might.

"We can't leave him," Rudy yelled.

"We have to," Theresa answered, "now."

Through shocks of red hair falling across his eyes, Rudy caught a glimpse of the oncoming zombie horde. Reluctantly, he let Theresa pull him away from the alley, and together they took off down the street, leaving their friend behind.

"It's a dead end," Brian yelled after them, "wait for me."

Rudy and Theresa looked over their shoulders in response but didn't slow. They caught sight of Brian emerging from the alleyway and meeting the zombies head on. Shots rang out from his Beretta, but the pack was already on top of him. His bloodcurdling scream ricocheted through the city as the dead swarmed over his large frame like a school of hungry piranha. They tore into him, ripping apart his limbs with their bare hands, sinking their rotted teeth into his face, neck, and torso.

As more zombies pounced and began fighting

131

over the last remnants of their fallen friend, Rudy and Theresa both stumbled. They almost lost their footing but somehow remained upright and kept running. Both of them now kept their eyes rooted on the escape route in front of them rather than on the horrible scene behind them.

Theresa's hysterical wails now replaced Brian's death screams in Rudy's ears. Hot tears welled in his eyes. His heart slammed against his ribcage with the panic of a death-row inmate facing the needle. A firestorm raged in his lungs as he desperately gulped for air. But on legs leaden with fatigue, he somehow kept running, still clutching the tree in a petrified grasp and pulling a sobbing Theresa along behind him.

The steel door to the underground compound loomed just ahead, and for the first time since starting this deadly footrace he felt hopeful that they just might make it to safety. It looked as though Brian's stupid mistake would save them in the end. It looked as though his friend's costly error had given them the time they needed to put just enough distance between themselves and the feeding zombies.

That's when Theresa's sweaty hand slipped from his grasp. She screamed, crashing to the pavement in a heap of skinned and bloody limbs. Behind her, a lone zombie rushed her for the kill.

Rudy skidded to a stop and reversed his course. He brandished the tree like a lethal weapon, shoving the trunk into the attacking zombie's horrid face. Grabbing her by the arm, he hauled Theresa to her feet and propelled her towards the steel door. The girl pounded on the door, screaming for help, while

Rudy fended off the foul creature with nothing more than a dying Christmas tree.

"Let us in," Theresa wailed, fists pounding on the door until they were raw and bloody, "let us in."

Rudy kept the tree between him and the zombie, swatting at its snapping jaws and blocking its reaching arms. Its maggot-riddled, leathery skin and its foul, rotting breath gagged him, sapped his strength and courage, but somehow he continued to fight the thing off.

"Let us in," Theresa screamed, pounding frantically.

"Let us in," Rudy echoed, seeing a pack of animated corpses storming down the street towards them.

The door abruptly opened. Theresa fell forward. Hands grabbed her, pulling her inside.

Rudy backed up toward the door, still fending off the lone zombie with the tree but unable to take his eyes off the oncoming storm. Suddenly someone grabbed him, pulled him backward, and slammed the door shut. But the zombie held onto the tree and came with him. Rudy, Christmas tree, and zombie landed in a tangled heap on the floor. The zombie, struggling to its feet, reared back like a poisonous viper and struck out, nipping Rudy on the little finger.

The next second, a shot boomed through the corridor. The zombie's head exploded, shrapnel of brain, skull, tissue, and blood splattering the steel door and wall.

Rudy lay on the floor, holding his injured hand with the other, wincing with pain and gasping for air. He shook red hair from of his eyes in time to see

Captain Dasher standing over him with a rifle trained on his head as if a bull's-eye were painted there.

"Get him to Klaus now," the captain commanded, "the tree too."

One soldier picked up the small tree and led the way, brown needles scattering on the floor behind him like breadcrumbs. Two more soldiers scooped Rudy up by the armpits and dragged him down the corridor and into the bowels of the compound. Captain Dasher followed, barrel of his rifle never wavering from Rudy's freckled face, finger ready at the trigger. Fellow survivors moved from their path, whispering and pointing fingers at the peculiar spectacle as they allowed the procession to pass.

Where they had taken Theresa, Rudy couldn't be sure. She was nowhere in sight, but he knew she was inside and safe. Right now, he was more worried about his own unpromising fate.

The soldiers delivered Rudy and the tree to the Med Lab. They yanked him to his feet and deposited him hard on one of the three exam tables. They threw the tree into a corner.

"You're dismissed," Klaus said, approaching the table.

The three soldiers took their leave as commanded, but Captain Dasher and his rifle remained.

Klaus stroked his white beard and ignored the captain. He said, "Rudy, I hear you were bitten."

Holding out his injured hand, Rudy nodded. Sweat beaded his brow. Hot tears welled in his eyes. A lump the size of his heart choked his throat. "Don't let him shoot me," he pleaded.

"No one's going to shoot you," Klaus assured him.

But Captain Dasher never lowered his weapon. "They never should've been out there," he growled.

"We'll discuss that later," Klaus snapped. He moved closer, examining the wound. "Just a nip," he mumbled.

Captain Dasher moved closer, as well. "Nip or not, he'll turn."

Klaus stroked his beard again. "Not if we can localize the infection in time."

"We can't take the chance," Captain Dasher insisted. "Look, the finger is already showing signs of infection."

Rudy's swollen pinky had turned a bright red. Black puss oozed from the bite wound.

Klaus nodded. "Then we better hurry, Captain. We're not going to shoot this young man outright. He deserves a chance."

"Does he?" Captain Dasher spat.

"Yes, Captain," Klaus insisted. "No matter what he's done, if we can save him then he deserves a chance.

"How're we going to save him?" the captain asked. "Cut the finger off?"

"No," Klaus said, "not yet anyway."

Tears and snot streamed down Rudy's face. His chest heaved. "What are you going to do?" he asked. "I'm not a lab rat. Tell me what you've got planned."

Klaus ignored him. He pulled a rubber strap from a drawer and wrapped it tightly around the base of Rudy's little finger.

Rudy winced and moaned as the throbbing in his

135

finger worsened with the tourniquet.

"Why not just cut the finger off?" the captain persisted with the idea of amputation as the answer.

"Cut it off," Rudy agreed, sobbing. "It's better than getting murdered." He gave the captain a teary yet cold stare. "Or worse becoming one of them," he added.

"Cutting the finger off won't stop the infection from getting into the bloodstream," Klaus explained as he set up an IV and stuck a needle into a vein on Rudy's hand. "I'd still need a tourniquet to keep the infection from spreading. Without the finger, I'd have no choice but to tie the tourniquet off at the wrist, and then you could lose the whole hand. No, this is our best chance. Hopefully, the combination of the tourniquet and the antibiotics in this IV will keep the infection localized in the finger. Once we're sure we've succeeded in doing that then we'll talk about cutting the finger off."

For the first time Rudy felt hopeful. His finger seemed a small price to pay to remain alive and infection free. He wiped tears and snot away with the back of his other hand. "You mean I might not change?"

Klaus patted Rudy on the shoulder. "That's what we're hoping. We'll know within twenty-four hours. If you haven't transformed by then, you're safe. Of course, you'll eventually have to lose the finger." Klaus shrugged. "But then what good would an undead finger do you?"

Rudy collapsed back onto the table and sighed.

Klaus cleared his throat. "Now, Rudy, tell me what you were doing out there."

Captain Dasher didn't give Rudy time to answer.

He picked up the small, brown tree in a stranglehold and shook it. "They went out for this," he yelled. "They risked their lives and the ultimate security of this compound for a half-dead Christmas tree."

Klaus raised bushy eyebrows. "They?" he asked.

Captain Dasher nodded. "And in the process the zombies got Brian. We lost a man and a weapon we couldn't afford to lose...and for what?" He threw the tree against the wall. In a spray of pine needles, it slid down the wall and collapsed onto the floor as if dead.

Klaus turned to Rudy. With a hard stare, he asked, "Just you and Brian went for the tree?"

Rudy sat up but lowered his eyes. Through a shock of red hair, he stared fixedly at the IV needle protruding from his hand.

Captain Dasher sidled up alongside Klaus and whispered, "They took Theresa with them."

Rudy glanced up at his benefactor.

A storm cloud passed over Klaus' face. His eyes went dark and cold. "Is she safe?" he asked, holding his breath.

"She's safe," Captain Dasher confirmed, "but no thanks to him."

Klaus slowly let the imprisoned air from his lungs. He leaned toward Rudy and whispered, "I'm going to save your miserable, little life. In return, Rudy, you'll stay far, far away from my daughter. Understand?"

Rudy opened his mouth to protest but nothing came out.

Klaus turned away and stormed out of Med Lab. "Keep a guard on him around the clock," he called.

Captain Dasher sneered at Rudy. "Yes, sir," he

said, pointing the barrel of his rifle at Rudy's frightened face.

◆◆◆

Two soldiers stood guard in the hallway, outside Med Lab. Rudy lay in the dark, alone with his thoughts and fears. A steady throb coursed through his dying finger. Periodically sharp pains joined the throb, streaking from tourniquet to fingertip like lightning bolts. Sweat beaded on his brow, red bangs plastered to his forehead. Chills swept through his body like a blustery wind. But rather than cooling him off, instead it fanned the wildfire burning just under his skin.

He was changing. He knew it. He had all the signs—fever, chills, aching joints and muscles. The tourniquet and antibiotics hadn't helped, hadn't saved him, and soon he would slip into a coma, only to awaken in a catatonic state, a flesh-eating zombie.

The thought gagged him. He sat up, choking with dry heaves, body convulsing and shivering. All around him, the room spun out of control. Seconds later, his world went pitch black.

◆◆◆

Rudy woke almost eighteen hours later, drenched in his own sweat. He rubbed the sleep from his eyes with his one good hand and moaned as he struggled into a sitting position.

Klaus stood at Rudy's bedside, a cold stare examining the patient. "It looks like you're through the worst of it," he said, voice hard. "Your fever broke a couple of hours ago. The fact that you're awake and still human is promising."

Rudy scowled at the good news. Yeah, he wasn't a zombie—yet, anyway—but the sight and smell of his finger disturbed him to no end. The pain had subsided and gunk no longer oozed from it. But the wound had crusted over in a thick and ugly, black scab. The skin around it had the pallor and scent of a corpse left out to rot in the noon-day sun. Flies buzzed around it, the putrefying flesh serving as both nourishment and nest.

Klaus caught him staring. "Not a pretty sight, is it?"

Rudy shook his head in disgust. "Cut it off," he pleaded.

Klaus shook his head. "Not just yet," he said, unhooking the IV.

Rudy gave him a questioning look. What he got back was a heartless, squinty-eyed stare. Screwing up his courage, he asked, "Why not cut it off? You said I was through the worst of it. I would've changed by now if I was going to, right?"

Klaus nodded in agreement. "I think we've managed to localize the infection," he said, releasing the tourniquet. "I don't think anymore of you is going to change."

"Then why not cut it off?" Rudy demanded.

Klaus leaned close, almost nose to nose. "Because I think you need to live with it for awhile," he growled. "I think it serves as a good reminder of just how stupid and irresponsible it was for you and Brian to take Theresa out into a zombie nest just for a Christmas tree." He straightened and backed away. "You're free to go," he said, with a cold shrug. "Maybe I'll cut it off if you come back in a day or two, after the holidays. Oh, just in case, I'd keep that hand elevated above your heart, if I were you."

Rudy blinked, fighting back hot tears. "You can't do that," he mumbled. "Cut it off now."

In answer, Klaus sneered. "Merry Christmas," he whispered and left the room.

Rudy couldn't believe what he had just heard, couldn't believe Klaus could be so cruel. He remained on the table in reflection, thoughts drowning in a stormy sea of fear and self-loathing. The thudding in his chest sounded like stampeding cattle, and he broke out in a cold sweat at the mere thought of living with an undead finger, even if only for a few days.

Staring at the little, brown Christmas tree left to die in the corner, he mumbled, "All I want for Christmas is my finger back...my life back."

Resigned, he let out a long, hitched sigh. He slid off the table onto wobbly legs—last night's battle against the zombie infection leaving him lethargic and weak. He wanted to hide the cursed finger somehow but was afraid not to keep it elevated above his heart as Klaus had suggested. So, with head bowed in humiliation and with hand held high as if it were a medal of honor rather than what he truly believed to be a shameful brand, he shuffled out of Med Lab and down the long, gloomy corridor.

The two armed guards stationed outside the door let him go but followed at a respectful distance. Along the way, people stopped and stared, pointing at him and whispering as he passed. Others heckled and jeered aloud, shaking fists and shouting obscenities after him. Children shot him frightened looks and ran the other way. Girls his own age cringed at the sight of him. A group of guys he had called friends just yesterday threw garbage at him. They all called him a murderer for the death of Brian and a monster for the undead finger that cursed his hand.

Rudy couldn't understand why the trailing guards hadn't stepped in to protect him. Guessing they hated and feared him as much as everyone else, he quickened his pace, frantic to get to the small, dark corner and the sleeping bag he called home. There, maybe he could hide his finger and his shame. There, he might be safe. What stopped him cold was the sight of Theresa and her group of friends, clustering together just outside the Mess Hall.

"Theresa," Rudy called. The urge to embrace her suddenly renewed his courage and helped propel him through the hostile crowd.

She saw him too. Her face went pale and her eyes widened. She held up her hands as if to ward him off and screamed, "Stay away from me, Rudy."

Like hitting a brick wall, her harsh words left Rudy woozy and confused. The armed guards moved in front of him, blocking his way. The corridor went deathly still and quiet, everyone's attention focused on the guy with the undead finger and the girl he loved.

"Don't come near me," Theresa yelled, pretty face contorted in disgust as she stared at Rudy's finger. "My dad said I should stay away from you."

Rudy opened his mouth to protest, but the crowd shouted him down.

"Yeah, leave her alone, you freak."

"Go join your zombie friends outside."

"We don't want you and your creepy finger

141

anywhere near us."

"Murderer…monster…creep…freak…"

Rudy turned to run but instead dropped to his knees. His shrieking cry echoed through the corridor. His beleaguered little finger turned bright red, twitching and convulsing as if in the throes of an epileptic fit.

Gunfire answered Rudy's cry, two shots booming through the corridor from the opposite side of the compound. People screamed in terror and started to scramble for safety. The two guards quickly flanked Rudy, eyeing both him and the crowd with wary glances.

Rudy's finger continued to tremble, radiating red as it did so. He cried out again, lightning bolts of pain streaking through the cursed thing.

From down the corridor, someone yelled, "Zombie."

Another shot boomed. Everyone screamed. The people who hadn't gotten out of the corridor now pasted their backs against the walls. A lone zombie dragged itself along the floor, black gunk trailing behind it like slime from a snail. It moaned woefully, wounded and dying. But somehow it kept going, sliding across the floor, slowly fleeing from the soldiers giving chase. The echo of boots thundered in the corridor as three soldiers raced up and surrounded the thing, rifles aimed and ready to blast it. Klaus and Captain Dasher followed hot on the soldiers' heels. They caught up just as the zombie collapsed, unable to go on.

"Wait," Klaus commanded.

"We need to finish it off," Captain Dasher insisted.

"Not yet, Captain," Klaus shot back, his gaze locked on Rudy.

Kneeling on the floor, Rudy's face contorted in pain. He cradled his injured hand within the other. His undead finger emanated a red glow and vibrated like a divining rod finding water.

Klaus surveyed the scene, stroking thoughtfully at his white beard. "Bring him closer," he instructed.

The two guards grabbed Rudy under the armpits, dragged him to his feet, and led him toward the dying zombie.

Rudy struggled to free himself but couldn't. "What're you going to do?" he asked, imagination running wild. "Stop...don't—"

The intense pain in his finger cut him short. He let loose the squeal of a tortured pig. His finger convulsed with maddening speed.

"Stop," Klaus commanded. "Now, back him slowly away."

The guards did as instructed.

Rudy's tortured cry died a slow death as they backed farther and farther away from the zombie. The redness subsided and the twitching calmed in his finger, as well.

Klaus grinned. "Terminate it," he commanded.

A round of gunfire from the three soldiers split open the zombie's head. Two of them picked up its feet and dragged the thing away by its ankles, leaving behind a smear of black zombie oil.

"What're you thinking?" Captain Dasher asked.

"I'm thinking we found our salvation," Klaus answered.

Captain Dasher shot his leader a confused look. "Salvation?" he asked. "Somehow this zombie penetrated our defenses. We're not even sure how or where it got into the compound, but if one found a way then others will soon follow. How can you talk of salvation?"

Klaus didn't answer. Instead, he went to Rudy. "Release him," he told the guards.

Rudy now stood with no help as the guards backed away. He kept his gaze locked on Klaus, unsure of what to expect, confused by this sudden turn of events. Just moments ago he thought they were going to feed him to the zombie. Now, a grinning Klaus approached him and put a gentle hand on his shoulder. He couldn't help but flinch at the sudden sign of affection.

"I hope you can forgive us, Rudy," Klaus said. "I hope you can forgive me."

Rudy shook red hair from his eyes and gave his leader a skeptical and defiant stare.

Klaus turned his attention to the throng of curious people surrounding them. "You've all heard me speak of the stronghold on the coast, an old army post turned into the last known remaining outpost of humanity," he said, voice ringing throughout the corridor.

The crowd murmured.

He held up a hand to silence them. "I've been in constant contact with them by radio," he continued, "and as many of you know it's been my longtime goal to somehow lead all of you from this retched underground existence, back out into the sunlight of day and the open, starlit sky of night."

The crowd stirred, whispering and nodding with anticipation.

Klaus continued, "The Pacific Ocean lends them

a naturally protected border. An electrified fence surrounds the entire perimeter. Strategically placed watchtowers are manned by armed soldiers. Old barracks serve as people's homes. People live above ground, in a viable community, protected and safe from the zombie horde. If we can make it there, life could be sweet again. There, we could comfortably wait for the zombies to exterminate themselves. Sooner or later, as their food supply dwindles, these horrible creatures will turn on themselves for food. But until that day comes, we could live free. Free to enjoy sunny days. Free to walk under a night sky. Free to move around on a hundred acres of protected land."

"But how do we get there?" someone in the crowd yelled.

"Rudy will take us there," Klaus called back.

Murmurs of disbelief ricocheted through the crowd.

Again, Klaus held up a silencing hand. "I believe that Rudy's finger will get us there safely. You all saw how it reacted to the zombie."

Captain Dasher shook his head. "How does that help us?" he asked.

"Don't you see," Klaus explained, "with his finger we can avoid the zombies. It'll warn us whenever we're close to danger."

Again the crowd stirred and murmured, this time in excitement rather than disbelief.

Klaus put a hand back on Rudy's shoulder. "What I'm trying to ask; Rudy, with your undead finger, won't you guide us to safety tonight?"

A hush fell over the compound as everyone held their collective breaths.

Rudy's jaw dropped. He couldn't believe what he had just heard. Somehow his curse would actually save them all? He stared down at his horrid finger before looking around at all the expectant faces.

Theresa sidled up alongside Rudy and took his good hand. He turned to look into the girl's blue eyes. Hope and adoration now replaced the disdain he had seen in them just moments ago.

"I know we don't have the right to ask," Klaus continued, "not after the way we…the way I…treated you. But we are asking, Rudy. What do you say…will you lead us to safety?"

Rudy knew he should be angry. He understood he had the right to feel bitter and vindictive. After all, just moments ago these very people had ridiculed and threatened him. But he felt none of those things.

Turning back to Klaus, Rudy grinned. "I'd be proud to lead the way," he said.

Theresa squeezed Rudy's hand and kissed him on the cheek.

Klaus let out a jolly laugh and slapped Rudy's back. "We leave tonight," he announced. "With Rudy's help and a little luck, we'll be in paradise by Christmas day."

A collective cheer resonated through the compound.

◆◆◆

That night, Rudy guided the survivors from the safety of their three-year, underground refuge out into the perilous, zombie-infested city. Klaus and Theresa followed close behind, he holding his daughter's hand in a tight grip, she carrying the

146

little, half-dead Christmas tree in her other hand. Armed guards flanked the procession. Captain Dasher brought up the rear. They kept to the side streets, stopping and hiding in the shadows whenever Rudy's finger warned of nearby danger. Three times they came close to being discovered by wandering, animated corpses. But thanks to Rudy, they managed to avoid any contact or conflict with the dead. Soon they found themselves on the outskirts of the city, traversing the open countryside toward the coast.

By sundown on Christmas day, a group of haggard survivors stood on a knoll, staring down at their salvation. The old army post looked well-protected and lively with human activity. Behind it, the Pacific Ocean stretched to the horizon. Beyond that stood a sky painted in deep purple and orange. By nightfall, they were all safe within the fort, welcomed with open arms and getting settled in their new home.

That night they gathered in the Mess Hall to celebrate Christmas and to pay tribute to their newfound freedom. At the center of the hall stood the little, brown Christmas tree, decorated with ribbons, bows, and strung popcorn. Somehow, the half-dead tree looked beautiful, like a Christmas miracle.

Klaus stood up before the throng and quieted them with raised hands. "Rudy," he called, "come up here."

Rudy and Theresa made their way through the crowd and stood at Klaus' side.

Klaus put an arm around Rudy's shoulder. "You did it," he said, with a jolly laugh. "You and that cursed finger of yours saved us and brought us to this glorious place. Son, we'll never forget what you've done for us. You'll indeed go down in history."

Theresa leaned in and kissed Rudy on the cheek.

The crowd cheered. Even Captain Dasher at the back of the room applauded.

Not knowing what to say, Rudy kept silent. But he couldn't stop the wide, proud grin from spreading across his freckled face. He couldn't believe his luck. He was a hero. What started out a curse had turned into a gift. For the first Christmas in three years they could celebrate without fear.

Klaus leaned close to Rudy's ear. Over the celebratory cheer of the crowd, he said, "Come see me in the morning. As a Christmas present, I'll cut off that finger for you." Then Klaus turned back to the crowd and bellowed, "Merry Christmas to all."

The roar inside the hall grew deafening.

Rudy leaned toward Theresa to kiss her, but a warning cut him short; an agonizing throb suddenly coursed through his finger. He bit his tongue, stifled a wail, and gaped at the twitching, red alarm on his hand.

Over the clatter, Rudy hollered, "Zombies."

The Halloween Box

The package arrived
On Halloween
Addressed to Fred
A box for me

I took it inside
On Halloween
And a feeling of dread
Came over me

Yet, I opened it up
My first mistake
Tears I shed
I began to shake

What I found
Gave me a fright
It wasn't quite dead
Yet it wasn't alive

Fred Wiehe

I rubbed my eyes
In disbelief
I looked again
But to no relief

The thing in the box
At me, it stared
Eyes beady and red
Sharp fangs it bared

Although it was small
Just a child
Still it was undead
Wicked and wild

From the box it lunged
Striking out at me
Hungry…unfed
Ready to feed

Blood it needed
To keep it alive
Blood from Fred
Oh my…Oh my

I retreated in fear
Ran for my life
To the bedroom I fled
To wake up my wife

Suzy sat up
Let out a scream
Jumped out of bed
"It must be a bad dream"

150

Holiday Madness

"No dream"
"No nightmare"
I quickly said
"Life really sucks…very unfair"
The vampire child
Now a large bat
Flew to the bed
That's where it sat

Suzy and I
Huddled as one
Our hearts filled with dread
We weren't having fun

Baring its fangs
The bat gave a sharp squeal
It needed to be fed
And we were the meal

Now my wife squealed
As the bat spread its wings
It flew at our heads
Intent on terrible things

It went for Suzy's throat
A terrible sight
It wanted her dead
I needed to fight

I grabbed the foul thing
Right in mid-flight
So it bit me instead
But saving my wife

151

Fred Wiehe

Fangs sunk into my throat
Bleeding me dry
Then Suzy fled
Giving this cry

"I'll be back"
"I won't go anywhere"
"Don't give up Fred"
"I'll kill it I swear"

My vision went black
I was losing the fight
Soon I'd be dead
Whether wrong, whether right

I heard Suzy scream
Then a squeal and a screech
The bat I did shed
It now collapsed at my feet

The vampire child
Lay on the floor
No longer undead
It had changed form

Into its back
An ice pick was stuck
Permanently dead
It ran out of luck

My wife held me
We were both still alive
Suzy and Fred
Would always survive

Bad Moon

Jake had been running to keep distance between Sarah and him. He now stopped and rested, panting hard. His ears pricked up. He cocked his head sideways as he listened.

Somewhere, an owl hooted. Horses in the distance neighed, snorted, and stomped their hooves. The hiss and stamping feet of a skunk warning off a predator joined the owl and horses in a bizarre kind of night song.

Jake wondered about what might be stalking the skunk. He worried about whether the predator might be large enough or dangerous enough to cause harm to Sarah or him.

Before his thoughts could darken too much, though, he coughed and gagged on the sudden foul odor that now mixed with the horse manure to choke the cold night air; apparently the skunk's warning hadn't worked, and whatever creature pestering it had gotten sprayed.

Holding his breath against the offensive smell, Jake turned his attention to the sky. An eerie mist drifted through the treetops and blanketed the night. Still, he could see the pale, full moon directly overhead, as if it were a light from heaven shining through a throng of ethereal angels. His gaze riveted to the sight and didn't pull away until he heard the steady clomping of a horse's hooves coming down the path toward him.

He moved to the shrubs at the edge of the path. There, he hid. He held his breath so as not to give away his position and quietly watched as the young girl rode past on her American Paint.

Sarah often came to the horse stables and the surrounding ten acres of wooded area late at night to ride.

Jake, in turn, came to watch over the girl—most nights anyway, like this night when the moon was full—both for Sarah's protection and admittedly because Jake liked seeing the girl atop the big horse. The sight of Sarah's lush, black hair bouncing about her pretty, pale face with each step of the horse and the way the girl's well-rounded curves moved as she posted in the saddle excited Jake to no end.

Secretly, Jake loved Sarah. They both attended Yuka High School and were in the same homeroom. Sarah was in Jake's algebra class too, and they had talked together a bit at school.

But Jake was sure the girl had no idea how he felt. And he was also sure that Sarah wouldn't understand his obsession of watching over her as she rode the trails late at night. Probably, the girl would think him a freak of some sort and be scared he meant her harm.

But he didn't. He only wanted to ensure Sarah's safety; there were dangers in the woods of which the girl had no knowledge, things she couldn't possibly comprehend.

Besides, even though Sarah looked healthy

enough—except for maybe a slight pasty complexion—she often missed school due to some sort of illness or another. Obviously, she had neither the strength nor the fortitude to fight off a would-be attacker of any sort. Obviously, she needed Jake to watch over her, to protect her.

Jake moved through shrubs with stealth, following Sarah and the horse the best he could.

"Easy," Sarah called to her horse, "easy, Big Bud."

The horse slowed from a canter to a steady trot.

Jake slowed, as well.

"Walk," Sarah commanded Big Bud.

The horse almost instantly slowed.

Jake stopped, keeping his distance, not wanting to be seen or heard. Besides, Sarah and Big Bud were heading back to the stables, and Jake didn't want the horses that were boarded there to catch his scent and give him away.

Something moved in the brush. Leaves rustled. Twigs cracked.

Big Bud shied at the sound, skipping sideways, snorting, stomping hooves.

"Ho, Bud," Sarah commanded. She came up out of her English saddle, almost losing her seat. But somehow she remained on the horse. She kept the horse in a tight circle with a one-rein stop—the rein pulled to her left hip, the horse's nose at her knee. But Big Bud fought Sarah all the way, snorting and stomping, chomping on the bit.

The thing in the brush quickened its pace, fighting through tangles of vines and shrubs, no longer concerned with noise.

Jake tried to circle around to get closer but

couldn't make it in time.

A wolfish howl blasted the night. A large, hairy beast sprang from the brush, onto the path. It landed on all fours, swinging its massive head about, growling and snarling, baring sharp canines.

Sarah gasped at the sudden sight of the hideous beast.

Big Bud snorted as he reared back on his hind legs and kicked at the air with his front hooves.

Miraculously, Sarah remained atop the horse.

But as Big Bud's front end came back to earth, the horse turned his butt, bucking and kicking his back legs at the wolf-like creature.

In the process, Sarah was thrown. She hit the ground with a hard thud. Somehow, though, she remained conscious and had enough sense to roll and barely dodge Big Bud's hooves as the horse now bucked and kicked frantically in all directions.

The wolfish beast was not so lucky. A hoof caught the creature in the ribcage, sending it flying through the air. It landed against a tree with a sickening thump, as if something inside it had broken on impact.

But even that didn't stop the hideous beast. As Big Bud took off running back to the stables in a cloud of dust, the wolf-like creature struggled onto its massive paws. It shook its head as if to clear the cobwebs away and stumbled about, getting its bearings. Although injured, its evil gaze again focused on Sarah. A menacing growl rumbled in warning.

Sarah scooted backwards. Her hands and feet propelled her as fast as they could while she still basically sat on her butt and faced the predator before her.

Meanwhile, the beast rose onto its hind legs, standing erect like a man. It staggered toward its prey. Massive jaws open. Sharp teeth exposed. Globs of thick saliva dripped from its maw.

Sarah didn't scream. Rather, she scooted back more until she blindly hit a tree, stopping her cold. Still, she didn't scream—even as the hungry beast advanced on her.

Maybe she knew the beast was hurt and thought it might drop dead at her feet before eating her. Maybe she was the bravest girl that ever lived.

Jake wasn't sure which. But he wasn't about to wait and see if the beast was going to die or if Sarah's courage would hold. Without thought for himself, he leaped from the bushes, onto the path, and positioned himself between the predator and the girl he secretly loved.

The beast stopped its advance and scrutinized the hero blocking its path. It growled—deep and guttural—not at all pleased at having its meal rudely interrupted.

Jake growled right back. He bared his teeth and rose onto his two hind legs, erect and ready to do battle.

Despite being injured, the predator now advanced with supernatural speed. It lunged at its challenger. Massive claws swiped the air, slashing into Jake's flesh.

Jake screeched in pain. Deep gashes across his chest oozed thick blood. Still, he counterattacked, ripping his own claws across his attacker's face and rupturing the thing's eyeball.

The beast howled in agony. Thick blood gushed

from its empty eye socket. But it didn't stop. Instead, it rushed Jake like an enraged bull.

Both Jake and the beast went down hard. A rumbling chorus of yowls, wails, and shrieks echoed through the woods. Locked in mortal combat, they tore and bit at each other, rolling in a massive tangle of slashing claws and gnashing teeth. Dust kicked up. Fur flew. Chunks of bloody flesh were spat out onto the ground. Blood flowed, staining the dirt.

Luckily, the beast's injuries from Big Bud's kick had weakened it, and Jake found himself on top and at a sudden advantage. Without hesitation and with supernatural speed of his own, Jake lunged at his adversary's throat.

The predator was now the prey.

The beast yelped as Jake bit down hard. Blood gushed forth, into Jake's mouth. The beast made a strange gurgling noise, and its body convulsed in the throes of death. But Jake didn't let go. He held on tight, using his strong jaws and sharp teeth to bear down and finish the thing off.

Jake finally released his death grip when the beast stopped moving and made no further noise. Blood dripped from Jake's open mouth as he stared down at his enemy.

What lay before him, however, was not the wolf-like creature that had attacked Sarah and that he had fought to the death. Instead, the naked body of a young man was sprawled out on the ground. In fact, Jake thought he recognized the young man as maybe a senior at Yuka High School.

Jake felt a slight pang of remorse as he looked down upon the bloody corpse; he had killed one of his own and maybe a classmate in the process, as well.

No matter, this werewolf had meant to eat Sarah and had to be stopped. Jake had had no choice but to intervene. He couldn't allow any harm to come to the girl he secretly loved.

Without further thought of guilt, Jake turned away. He faced Sarah who still sat with her back to the tree.

The girl neither looked frightened nor horrified by the strange turn of events she had just witnessed. Rather, she stared with idle curiosity at both the bloody young man lying dead on the path and the werewolf who had just saved her life.

Jake crept toward the girl on all fours. He didn't stop until he was face to face with his love.

Sarah never flinched. She scrutinized the werewolf and gazed into his eyes with an icy, blue stare.

"Jake?" Sarah whispered in sudden recognition.

It was Jake who flinched as Sarah reached out and touched wiry fur.

"It is you Jake, isn't it?" Sarah asked in wonder, petting the werewolf.

Jake couldn't believe that Sarah recognized him just by his eyes. He moved closer and nuzzled the girl. Maybe Sarah secretly felt the same.

Dare he hope?

"Jake, you shouldn't have," Sarah whispered. "I'm not worth it."

Jake licked Sarah on the cheek as if to say she was wrong; she was everything.

Then the werewolf turned away. He trotted to the bloody body on the path. Grabbing the dead man's arm, Jake dragged his victim away, disappearing into the dark woods.

♦♦♦

The next morning, Jake thought about skipping school. He wondered how he could face Sarah after last night. After all, she knew Jake's secrets—all of them.

Jake imagined Sarah to be really freaked out about now; not only had the girl found out that she was being watched and apparently obsessed over, she also found out that this secret admirer and part-time stalker was a werewolf.

Yeah, last night—during that instance of recognition, during that instance of petting—Jake thought maybe Sarah felt something not unlike affection or fondness. But after a night of consideration and in the light of day, would the girl feel anything other than revulsion and loathing?

After all, she had seen Jake kill.

Jake not only worried about how Sarah felt but whether she would tell. If she did, who would she tell? And would anyone believe her?

Last night, after dragging away the body, Jake had eaten most of it. Then he scattered what was left throughout the woods. Vultures and other animals would certainly take care of the rest. The young man would be just one more missing teenager, one more unsolved mystery.

Even so, Jake had thought about running away. But what would that accomplish? He had no money. He had nowhere to go.

Besides, if Sarah had already told someone—and they believed the girl or even suspected her story might be true—then the police would've certainly been at Jake's home this morning to arrest

160

him.

So Jake had to go under the assumption that Sarah hadn't told anyone yet. With that being the case, and having no money and nowhere to go, then skipping school today would only prolong matters. He had to face Sarah sooner or later.

He had to know if the girl planned to tell.

Still, hurrying to school wasn't a priority either.

Jake slung a backpack laden with books over his shoulder. He sauntered to school, in no hurry to get there. Overhead, dark clouds buried the sun under a dreariness that reminded him of the gloom and misery brewing within his own heart and soul, as if the sky mirrored his darkest feelings. Lost in thought, he arrived fifteen minutes late. Everyone else had already gone inside for homeroom attendance.

Everyone, that is, except Sarah.

Sarah waited, sitting on the front steps. She stood at the sight of Jake's approach.

Jake faltered. He hesitated slightly and for an instant thought about retreating, before he bravely continued on toward the girl waiting for him. But with each step, it seemed as if a battle waged within him: Blood pounded in his ears. His heart slammed against the inside of his chest. His throat constricted as if being strangled. Even though it was a cloudy and sunless day, sweat trickled down his back and soaked his underarms.

Besides all that, his mind was in a panic.

Maybe Sarah had told someone, after all. Maybe this was a trap of some sort.

Jake scanned the surrounding campus.

There was no sign of anyone else, such as the

161

police or even school administration for that matter.

No, like Jake thought earlier, Sarah probably hadn't yet told anyone. If she had, then she wouldn't be waiting alone.

Jake studied the girl's pretty face as he got closer. But her blue eyes were an icy stare and her expression unreadable. There was no telling how the girl was about to react.

Jake stopped just a foot or two away. He stared at Sarah, unable to speak, unable to find any suitable words as an explanation for last night.

Sarah stepped closer, now just inches away. She looked up into Jake's face, examining him as a scientist might a lab specimen.

"There's no full moon tonight, right?" Sarah asked.

Still unable to find his voice, Jake just shook his head no in response.

Even though Sarah smiled, her face remained expressionless, her gaze icy.

Jake didn't know what to think, what to expect.

Sarah said, "Meet me in the woods by the stables."

"Huh?" Jake asked, uncomprehending.

Sarah turned away. She walked up the cement steps to the front doors of the high school.

Jake gaped after the girl.

Did he hear right?

Sarah opened the door but stopped before going inside. She turned back and stared at Jake with those icy, blue eyes. Over her shoulder, she said, "Ten o'clock…you know where."

With that, Sarah strolled through the door and let it close behind her.

Jake stood, frozen to that spot. He gawked at the front door of the school as if Sarah still stood there.

What had just happened? Did the girl he'd been obsessing over for so long just ask him out?

A smile crept across his face. The battle that had been waging inside him called a cease fire.

Rather than despise him for being less than human. Rather than be frightened of him for being a killer. Rather than turn him into the police. Sarah just asked him out.

What had he been so worried about?

Still smiling, Jake bounded up the steps and hurried into school.

◆◆◆

The eerie mist that last night had drifted through the treetops now settled low to the ground. Rather than resembling ethereal angels in the sky, the low-floating fog on this night looked more like ghostly specters haunting the woods. The waning moon was nowhere to be seen.

Jake hunched his shoulders against the chill. With hands plunged deep inside the pockets of his jacket, he maneuvered through the woods. Even in human form, his night vision was better than most people, and he could still move with some animalistic skill and cunning, as well. Therefore, he had no need to use the paths and could remain discreet in his approach.

He stopped in some thick brush, just short of the path where he was to meet Sarah. From that vantage point, through the ghostly mist, Jake could see the girl already there, waiting. She stood next to Big Bud while the horse grazed on some grass along the edge of the path.

The sight of Sarah set Jake's heart to pounding, like a car battery being jumpstarted. He couldn't catch his breath either—which was visible in the cold night air. His stomach did somersaults at the mere thought of holding the girl's hand or better yet being in her arms.

Would this long, sought-after fantasy finally come true?

Jake could feel his hands tremble and sweat inside his jacket pockets. Worried that he might wake from this dream before it had a chance to play out, he took a deep breath and stepped from the brush, onto the path.

Sarah turned toward the sound of Jake's approach. Upon seeing her visitor, she said, "I was starting to worry."

Jake stood a few feet away, frozen, unable to move closer. He said nothing.

Sarah stepped toward him. "I know you can speak. I've heard you at school." She chuckled.

Jake cleared his throat. "Don't want to say anything stupid," he said.

Sarah kept moving steadily forward. "You mean like that?"

Jake smiled in spite of himself. He could feel his face burn with embarrassment. Nodding, he said, "Yeah."

Sarah stopped just short of touching Jake. Her icy, blue gaze studied the young man's face. "Last night," she said, "you shared your secret. Tonight, I want to show you mine."

Jake gave the girl a questioning look.

Sarah moved even closer. She wrapped her arms around the young man's neck. Jake in turn wrapped his arms around Sarah's back. Their bodies now pressed together.

If possible, Jake's heart pounded even harder; his dream—his fantasy—was actually coming true.

Sarah put her lips to Jake's ear. She whispered, "Do you want to know my secret?"

Jake shivered. "Yeah," he murmured.

Sarah exposed sharp fangs. She plunged them deep into Jake's throat.

Jake gasped and moaned. Unexpected and sudden, Sarah's bite stung and felt pleasurable all at the same time. As if under a spell, Jake at first willingly succumbed to the girl's advances, not fully comprehending the implication of the bite and Sarah's secret.

But as the girl continued to suck and drain blood, Jake soon realized his mistake.

By then, however, it was too late. The young man already felt weaker, woozy in the head, and wobbly on his legs. He groaned miserably and dropped to his knees.

Sarah held on tight. She dropped to her knees, as well. Her fangs still penetrated her victim's throat.

Jake tried to fight back. But he had lost too much blood. Consciousness was slipping away. His mind stood on the precipice of life, and the abyss of death called his name. He could hear it.

Sarah finally removed her fangs and released her victim.

Jake fell to the ground with a dull thump.

Sarah leaned forward.

Through blurred vision, Jake could see the vampire's leering face, her bloody fangs.

"You killed one of your own, Jake," Sarah

whispered. "How could you?"

"I…loved…you," Jake croaked.

"And that's what killed you," Sarah said. "It blinded you to what the other werewolf already knew. That's why it hunted me." Licking blood from her lips, Sarah stood. "I could never kill one of my own. You shouldn't have either, Jake." She stared down at Jake without pity, blue eyes like ice. "You shouldn't have saved me. I told you; I'm not worth it."

Turning away, Sarah went to Big Bud. She put her boot into a stirrup, grabbed the horse's mane, and pulled herself up and into the saddle.

Jake groaned in agony and misery.

"I…loved you," he croaked again.

The blurry image of Sarah atop her horse, riding away, was the last thing he saw.

The Three Wolf Men

Father Joseph Christy sat at a small, wooden table, deep in prayer. Hobgoblins of wind beat against the door and rattled the windows. They hissed with menace and panted with hunger through the eaves. They swooped across the roof, wings and talons scraping wooden shingles. They shook the cabin as if with a primal need to get inside at him, ensnare him within their cold, coiling currents.

Inside, the fireplace was alive and hot with dancing flames. Dried wood and pine cones crackled and spat back at the advancing hobgoblins that beat against the windows and door. Three oil lamps dispersed throughout the room protected the priest from the oncoming night. Dusky shadows and lamp glow fought each other in hand-to-hand combat across the floor, up the walls, and onto the ceiling—the eternal struggle between darkness and light.

The ululating cry of a hurt animal ricocheted across the valley, a stray bullet of pain and suffering. It startled Father Joseph from his prayers; he had never heard anything like it before. The sheer shrill of it indicated excruciating agony. But it cut short as quickly as it had started.

Father Joseph pushed up out of the wood-framed chair. With legs numb from sitting so long, he staggered across the floor like a landlubber crossing the deck of a ship that sailed a storm-ravaged sea. He stared out the porthole at an ocean of snowdrifts rather than crashing waves. No new snow fell, and a sailor's moon—full and bright—lit up the clear sky and cast an eerie glow upon the forested landscape. But the invisible hobgoblins kicked angrily at the snow, creating a white blanket as thick as sea fog.

He squinted through the swirling snowflakes, his gaze settling on his parked SUV. The Ford Explorer still sat protected under the carport where he had parked it, just a few yards from the cabin. His gaze then struck out across the valley's snow-laden floor, toward the distant, tree-lined horizon and the mountainous terrain beyond, in search of whatever had cried out in the night. Within the moon glow, three dark, indistinguishable shapes emerged from the forested hills, out into the surrounding whiteness in the valley. They moved oddly, sometimes erect like men, sometimes on all fours like beasts, but none moved as if hurt.

It was Christmas Eve, but those three certainly weren't the Three Wise Men following the Christmas star. They weren't Jesus, Mary, and Joseph looking for a warm place to sleep either. More likely they were the three bears—Papa, Mama, and Baby hunting for food.

But didn't bears hibernate in the winter?

Father Joseph wasn't sure. Anyway, whatever had made that God-awful noise had stopped. It was either dead or had not been as hurt as the cry had first indicated.

Shrugging, the priest turned away. Pins and needles now attacked his legs as circulation returned. He crossed the cabin, stopping at the fireplace to throw on more dried wood. The fire spat sparks at him as he retreated back to the table and his prayers.

He had come to this desolate, mountain cabin in the middle of nowhere three days ago. It had started snowing almost the second he arrived and hadn't stopped until tonight.

The invisible hobgoblins banged on the windows and moaned through the eaves. The entire cabin shook as if this was the cabin of the three little pigs and the big bad wolf was trying to blow it down.

Half-heartedly, Father Joseph resumed his prayers. But a white haze of doubt swirled in his head like the snow outside, blanketing his mind within a mind-numbing blizzard. He came here—to this two-room cabin owned by his best friend, Father Tim—to search his soul, pray for guidance, and to somehow regain lost faith. But even as he prayed, he doubted anyone was listening; he doubted God's existence.

Having joined the priesthood fresh out of high school, almost thirteen years ago, he had given his entire life to the service of God. How could he now doubt all that he had believed?

Because despite all his prayers, God let his sister's baby die.

Tears welled in the priest's eyes at the mere thought of his newborn nephew's death. His prayers

169

choked in his throat. He couldn't go on.

Outside, blustery hobgoblins beat against the windows, scurried across the roof, and whistled through the eaves, playing their invisible games. The fire spat at him as if in disgust.

In a few hours it would be Christmas, a celebration of Christ's birth. But the priest could only think of his nephew's death—a promise of a life that would never be.

A loud thud at the front door startled Father Joseph from his dark thoughts. No gust of wind had made that sound. Something or someone must've hit the door.

But who or what?

Even in his depressed state of mind, he remembered the pain-ridden cry in the night. Could the wail and the thud at his front door be connected? He also remembered the three dark shapes emerging from the forest. Had they come to visit? And just what were they?

He stood on shaky legs. Remembering Father Tim kept a revolver, he stumbled to a desk. Opening the top drawer, he found inside a .38 Special and a box of ammo. He took both out and returned to the table. He loaded six rounds then retrieved a lantern and tip-toed to the door. Opening it just a crack, a hobgoblin blast of arctic wind and a fine crystalline spray bit him in the face. But it was the sight of the naked woman lying on the doorstep in the snow that shocked the priest frigid with shivering dread. Next to the woman lay a bundle of blankets.

Forgetting his own safety, Father Joseph threw the door open wide and hurried to the woman. He hunkered down next to her, set down the lantern, and felt for a pulse. She felt like a block of ice to the touch. But he found a weak pulse. She barely hung onto life. Deep gouges and bite marks covered her blue-pale skin, bloody icicles forming around the wounds.

He thought of the ululate cry. Could this woman have made what had sounded like a hurt beast? And how did she get out in the middle of nowhere, in the middle of a snowstorm, unclothed, on Christmas Eve? More important, what had attacked her?

The priest again remembered those three indistinguishable shapes he had seen emerging out of the forest. He remembered how they had walked both erect and on all fours. Were they bears? Had they attacked her? If so, how'd she manage to get away?

Even if he discovered the answers to those questions, it didn't explain how she got out here in the first place or why she wore no clothes.

Shoving the revolver in his waistband, Father Joseph picked up the woman as he would a baby. He carried her through the front room, into the back room, and put her in bed. After covering the woman with multiple blankets, he turned and hurried back outside to the bundle waiting on his doorstep. To his shock, the bundle moved. Picking it up, he discovered a child wrapped inside, a baby not more than one-year old, if that.

If the frigid air or finding a naked woman on the doorstep hadn't shaken the priest enough, the fact that he now held a tiny baby in his arms did.

The child was semiconscious, near frozen to death, but breathing and moving.

Father Joseph took a quick scan of the

countryside, searching for the three mysterious figures, but there was no sign of them within the swirling blanket of snow being kicked into the air.

Hurrying inside with the baby, the priest closed the door and this time barred it, as well. He hadn't bothered before but these strange events both heightened his caution and his senses. Danger lurked outside, he was sure of it. Whatever those things were, they had attacked this poor woman and her baby. And chances were the beasts would come to finish what they had started.

Father Joseph carried the baby to the back room, but the mother remained unconscious. She was too near death. There was nothing to be done for her but to keep her warm under the blankets in her wait for God to take her.

Sitting down on the bed, the priest blessed the dying woman with the sign of the Cross and prayed to God for forgiveness of her sins, to accept her into His eternal bosom. The woman's fate was now in the Lord's hands.

With God's work done, the priest took the baby to the front room, scooted a chair toward the fireplace, and sat down in front of the roaring fire. He opened the blankets slightly and discovered the baby naked within the bundle.

Why would both mother and baby be out in a snowstorm unclothed?

He just couldn't bend his mind around that phenomenon.

Placing a hand on the baby's chest, the priest felt a strong, steady heartbeat. He smiled.

The mother had done her job. She had kept her child safe and alive at peril to her own life.

172

Father Joseph parted the blankets further to check the baby's gender. "A boy," he whispered.

The fire spat and crackled in response.

He wrapped the boy back up, thoughts full of his dead nephew. He held the baby close, hoping both the fire and his own body heat would bring the boy around. Although, the heartbeat was strong, and the baby moved in response to being touched, the boy's eyes remained closed, and he made no sound.

"What should I call you?" Father Joseph asked the baby but of course never expected an answer. "My best friend's name is Tim—Father Tim. I think maybe I'll call you that." He laughed for the first time in months. "Oh, not the Father part…just Tim, like Tiny Tim in A Christmas Carol." He laughed again and said, "God bless us…everyone."

Outside, gunfire of beastly howls blasted the night. The echoes of them shot across the valley and ricocheted about the snowcapped ridges.

Father Joseph jumped to his feet. He held the baby close and pulled the .38 from his waistband.

From the bedroom, glass shattered.

He swung both his attention and the gun's barrel toward the doorway and braced for an attack. But only cold air charged out.

Mumbling the Lord's Prayer, the priest cautiously inched his way toward the bedroom, his gun hand wracked with tremors. At the doorway, he peeked around the corner, afraid of what he might find. Cold air met his face and ruffled his hair.

Someone or something had broken the window; shards of glass littered the floor.

Worse, the bed was empty. Bloody blankets and smears of blood across the floor and up the wall to the window was all that remained of the frozen woman. Something had gotten in and taken her.

But what?

Using the barrel of the gun, Father Joseph crossed himself and backed out of the room. He put his back against the wall, afraid of being snuck up on from behind. His heart slammed against his ribcage like a psychopath beating at prison bars. His breath caught·in his throat as if it were solid mass rather than air. He held the baby to his chest. He didn't know what to do or where to go.

It wasn't a bear that had taken the woman, he felt sure of that. The howling outside right before something smashed the window sounded like wolves. But wolves couldn't have gotten in the window and carried a full-grown human back out again, could they?

But then what had?

Another round of howling gunfire blasted the night. It came from all sides as if surrounding the cabin. And he was wrong; the howls didn't sound like wolves exactly but rather evil, otherworldly, like the screams of demons.

Father Joseph prayed for forgiveness and help. He knew he didn't deserve it, having lost faith these past few months. But for the baby's sake, the priest implored the Holy Trinity for understanding and protection; the baby's survival depended on him staying alive. And although he didn't fear death, even at the hands of unknown evil, he truly wanted to live.

Outside, echoes of howls mixed with keening shrills and guttural growls. Death definitely stalked the countryside and surrounded the cabin. Whatever those things—those creatures—were, they sounded consumed by ravenous hunger. The evil things probably had eaten the poor woman, but she hadn't been enough to satisfy their beastly appetites.

Father Joseph held the baby close; he and the child were next on the menu. He felt sure of that.

Quickly, he crossed the room to the small table, retrieving the box of ammo. Hurrying back to the wall, he again put his back to it. He hunkered down, placing the baby on the floor. Opening the box of ammo, the priest blessed the bullets with the sign of the Cross. He emptied the revolver's cylinder, six bullets in his palm, and blessed those as well.

Why? He wasn't sure. Instinct or maybe renewed faith told him to do it, nagged at him to do it.

Working quickly, he reloaded the gun and grabbed a handful of bullets, stuffing them into the pocket of his jeans. He picked the baby back up in his arms and once again stood with his back to the wall, facing the front door, blessed ammo in both his gun and pocket, the rest in the box at his feet, ready for the imminent onslaught, praying to God for the courage to face this unknown peril.

But the wails and cries echoing through the valley rattled his nerves, shook his senses, and whittled away at his resolve.

Why didn't they just attack?

The window closest to the door suddenly imploded, glass shattering, shards flying through the air like shrapnel. A huge, hairy beast scrambled through the opening. It landed on all fours— growling, snarling, baring teeth. Slowly it rose onto its two hind legs. Standing erect like a man, it was at least seven feet tall. Gray, wiry hair covered it from head to toe. The wolf-like head on its shoulders was oversized, hideous. Massive jaws snapped together, sharp canine teeth gnashing and globs of thick saliva dripping in anticipation of a feast. Its eyes glowed red. As if the devil's fire burned within it.

Father Joseph froze like the ice-covered tundra outside. Proof that the devil existed stood before him. Yet, he couldn't believe what he saw. How could anything so horrible actually exist in God's world? His eyes had to be playing tricks on him. He had to be hallucinating. This couldn't really be happening. This thing before him couldn't be real. Wolf men only existed in B movies and bad horror books. They didn't walk among the living.

The beast let loose with a guttural growl. Still erect, it slowly moved closer, the sharp, curved claws on each toe clicking against the hardwood floor with each step. It seemed in no hurry to kill them, even oddly cautious. Then, just a few feet away, it took a half-hearted swipe with a massive front paw, its sharp claws just inches from skinning the priest's face.

Father Joseph flattened himself against the wall, raising the gun to take aim. The wolf man eyed it with a strange curiosity, as if it somehow knew mere bullets would do it little if any harm. The bullets weren't silver as legend and lore insisted.

But even better, they'd been blessed by a servant of God.

The first blast from the revolver hit the wolf man high in the shoulder. It didn't rock the beast backward, but the thing still cried out in agonizing pain and shock. A strange mixture of dark blood and

176

black smoke exuded from the wound, as if the blessed bullet not only wounded it but burned its flesh too.

Encouraged, the priest wasted no time. He blasted the thing again, hitting it squarely in the chest. This time the beast staggered backwards, keening loudly as if lamenting its own death.

Father Joseph shot it again and again, pulling the trigger even after the cylinder clicked empty.

Blood and smoke pouring from its wounds, the beast went down hard, panting, hissing, giving one last guttural snarl before death extinguished the burning light in its evil eyes.

The priest still pointed the gun at the thing on the floor, finger pulling the trigger in reflexive fear, hammer clicking on empty chambers. He didn't stop until the beast on the floor no longer existed. In its place lay a naked man in a pool of dark-red blood, death having transformed the beast back into human form.

"Just a man," Father Joseph muttered, "a man who sold his soul to the devil."

He looked down upon his adversary not with triumph or fear but with pity. The wolf men had underestimated this servant of God and sent only one to take care of the dirty business of killing him and taking the baby. He felt sure they wouldn't make the same mistake twice.

"Forgive him his sins, oh Lord," the priest prayed. He blessed the dead man with the sign of the Cross.

But he had little time for either mourning the dead or regretting the kill. Something sounding like a battering ram slammed into the front door,

177

splintering the doorjamb, breaking the wooden bar in two. The door exploded inward, large slivers and jagged fragments of wood soaring dangerously about the room as if a bomb had gone off. By some miracle none found their way to the baby or to the priest.

But good luck ended there.

As if blown through the doorway with the biting wind, two large wolf men sprang into the room: the larger of the two pure black, the smaller one silver and white. They landed on all four paws, snarling, baring canines, globs of drool dripping from their muzzles, eyes blazing red. They swung their huge heads back and forth, growls resonating with beastly fury.

Father Joseph aimed the gun at the big black one and pulled the trigger, hammer clicking against the empty chamber. "Sweet, Jesus...no," he mumbled.

Fear had caused him to make two fatal errors—emptying the gun into the first wolf man and not immediately reloading afterward.

The black wolf man curled its upper lip as if in a mocking sneer. It rose onto its hind legs. Standing erect, it slowly came towards its prey, claws clicking against the hardwood floor, red eyes focused on the baby cradled in the priest's arm. The silver one remained behind, still on all fours, watching, waiting, strangely cautious against one man with an empty gun.

With the baby in one arm and the gun in the other, Father Joseph found it impossible to get to the bullets in the pocket of his jeans and reload. Instead, he shoved the gun into his waistband and slowly backed away from the advancing wolf man, toward

178

the fireplace. When he felt the fire's heat on the back of his legs, he turned quickly and raced the wolf man the last few remaining steps to the fire. He got there first, but the beast was hot on his heals, claws viciously racking down his back, shredding his shirt, ripping into his flesh.

Crying out in pain, the priest still managed to get his hand on a burning piece of wood. He swirled around with it, shoving the flame into the wolf man's hairy face just as its massive jaws snapped at his own face.

The wolf man shrieked as the fire burned into flesh and ignited black fur. In seconds, its entire head was ablaze, spreading quickly down its huge body, instantly turning the evil creature into a blazing inferno. It whirled about the room, a fiery tornado, ricocheting off furniture and walls, igniting curtains, knocking over oil lamps, spreading its hot flames throughout the cabin, destroying everything in its path. The thing's pitiful, ululate cries reverberated off walls and ceiling.

The silver wolf man hopped about, trying to avoid contact with its fellow beast, looking as if it played a perverse game of dodge the fire ball. Finally, it managed to escape out the door, disappearing into the night.

Father Joseph tried to get to the box of ammo he'd left on the floor, but the blazing tornado and the rapidly spreading fire prevented him from getting across the room. Besides, black smoke and the acrid odor of burnt hair and flesh choked the air. He had to get the baby out of there before the boy's tiny lungs were irreparably damaged.

Stumbling across the room, the priest lunged for

179

the open doorway, losing his footing outside and slipping in the snow. He landed on his back, baby still cradled in his arm as the blaze hit the discarded box of ammo. He rolled over, protecting the baby with his body while what sounded like a war exploded from inside the cabin. He only struggled to his feet after the last round boomed into the night.

Once on his feet, he plowed through the snow to the SUV, digging into his pocket for the car keys, pulling them free, and hitting the unlock button as he ran. The SUV beeped and blinked its lights at him as the roof of the cabin crashed down, the fiery blaze engulfing the last of Father Tim's winter getaway.

Once the priest got the car door open, he placed the baby on the passenger seat, put his back against the open doorway, and scanned the valley for any sign of the silver wolf man. He saw nothing. But the biting wind blurred his vision with tears; he didn't trust his eyes. He was sure danger still lurked out there, in the dark.

Panted plumes of icy breath blasted out of his open mouth as he drew the gun from his waistband and fished in his jeans' pocket for bullets. He pulled out a handful, but his frozen fingertips fumbled with the bullets and the gun's cylinder. Somehow, he managed to get three rounds loaded into the chamber, the rest spilling into the snow or bouncing under the SUV. He went back into his pocket in search of more but found it empty.

"No," Father Joseph muttered.

He had no time to search through the snow or under the car. Three rounds would have to be enough—like the Holy Trinity.

"Lord, help me," he prayed.

After shutting the door, he hurried around the front of the SUV to the driver's door. His hand reached to open the door just as the wolf man hit him in the back. The impact slammed him into the car and sent him and the silver beast head over heels, limbs tangled, tumbling into the snow. The two adversaries wrestled themselves free of each other, coming up on their haunches face to face.

With jaws open wide, canines bared, the wolf man lunged.

Miraculously, Father Joseph held fast to the gun. He brought the barrel up and fired, hitting the horrid beast in the throat while in mid-air. The thing fell on top of him, smashing him into the snow. He pushed it off, struggling to regain his footing. Once on his feet, he took aim and fired again, hitting the wolf man in the back of the head while it lay helplessly on the ground.

The snow surrounding the beast turned dark as midnight under the moon glow. Black smoke poured from the wolf man's gaping wound. But it remained a beast, and its hairy body convulsed with shallow, ragged breath.

With the toe of his boot, the priest kicked the dying beast over onto its back. Father Joseph aimed the gun at where he supposed a wolf man's heart should be. He couldn't leave it to suffer. Besides, what if it somehow survived? He also couldn't live with himself if anyone else in the future died for his mistake now.

"Die!" he cried, pulling the trigger.

The blast echoed through the valley. The bullet smashed into the wolf man's chest. Within seconds, a naked woman lay in the bloody snow where the beast had been, a smoky haze covering her like a funeral shroud for just a second before dissipating on a stiff wind.

Father Joseph didn't linger to consider the gender of the dead body at his feet. He turned his back to it, stomping through the snow to the SUV. He climbed behind the wheel, slamming the car door shut behind him. Setting the .38 on the console, he cranked the engine to life and scooped up the baby from the passenger seat, settling the boy comfortably on his lap. After backing out from under the carport, the SUV then shot forward, running over the body for good measure, leaving behind the burning cabin and death.

"Thank you, Lord," Father Joseph prayed. "Thank you for saving me and little Tim."

He cranked up the heat as he drove across the valley, looking for some sign of the road. He tried to remember where it should be, but all he could see stretching out before him in the headlight beams was a vast whiteness.

"And thank you for four-wheel drive too," he said with a smile.

Not being able to find the road wasn't going to darken his mood. He was alive. With God's help, he had slain evil and saved the baby. He had a renewed faith in God, in himself, and in a life devoted to the church. Somehow, he would make amends for losing faith. He'd find a way. Life seemed sweet again.

The baby stirred in his lap and started to cry; Tim had finally regained full consciousness.

Father Joseph's smile and good feelings both

182

faded, though, as the boy's cry turned into what sounded like a rumbling growl. The priest parted the blankets to check the baby but instead found a little, hairy beast. The thing stared up with beady, red eyes, snarling and baring teeth.

"Sweet, Jesus!" Father Joseph screamed.

He reached for the gun on the console as the wolf baby lunged up and sank its sharp, tiny canines into his wrist, ripping away a chunk of flesh into its mouth and hungrily feeding.

Blood gushed from the wound as the priest lost control of the SUV, fishtailing and spinning out of control, smashing sideways into a tree. On impact, he hit his head on the window next to him, spider-webbing the glass. But somehow he remained conscious, shaking the cobwebs away even though the crash had opened a gash on his head and blood poured from the bite wound on his wrist. Though groggy and vision blurred, he immediately noticed the passenger door standing wide open.

How?

He couldn't imagine. But the little beast was making good its escape, running on all fours, up a snow-covered hill.

Father Joseph grabbed the gun, rolled across the console and passenger seat, and spilled out onto the snow. He struggled onto his knees, groaning at the effort and the pain. Under the moon glow, he watched in horror as the wolf baby ran up the hill toward a waiting pack of ten to fifteen beasts.

The three wolf men hadn't been trying to kill or eat the baby at all. They had been sent by the pack to get it back. That's why they'd been hesitant to attack. They hadn't wanted to risk harm to one of their own.

Had the mother stolen it, not wanting to raise it in the pack? Was this wolf baby their Christ child, their Messiah?

Father Joseph would never know, didn't want to know.

The wolf baby reached the pack, but the wolf men remained rooted to their spot, watching the priest, as if waiting for something.

What were they waiting for?

Father Joseph stared down at his bleeding wrist. He'd been bitten.

Were they waiting for him to become one of them?

Still holding the gun, he sat back on his legs, beaten.

Frigid air smacked his face. Icy breath escaped from his mouth. He stared at the heavens, helpless, the full moon mocking him.

He had to prevent himself from becoming something horrid and wicked; he refused to serve the devil.

Hand trembling, he raised the gun to his head, barrel firmly planted against his temple, resigned to his fate.

"God, forgive me," he prayed.

He pulled the trigger. The hammer clicked against empty chamber.

Father Joseph screamed in disgust at the full moon. He dropped the gun into the snow.

God had forsaken him, after all.

He again screamed at the moon.

And then the scream turned into an animalistic wail.

184

Trick or Troll

Pitch black surrounded him. Jerry sat on the floor, in the corner of his kitchen, knees drawn up under his chin. He wrapped both arms in a bear hug around his legs.

He couldn't see his front door from where he sat in the dark, but he knew the little beastie was back. It had returned…probably had never left. He didn't have to see it. He felt its presence—greasy and slick—in the pit of his stomach. Not only that but an inexplicable, eerie draft slithered like a snake along the back of his neck, gooseflesh attacked his scalp, whispers jabbered incessantly within his head, and the air turned heavy, hard to breathe, as if it were polluted by black soot.

Yeah, he knew the signs, the beastie was there all right, crouching at the threshold of his home, lurking, lying in wait.

God said to Cain, "Sin crouches at the door."

Well, Jerry believed it; sin—in the form of a troll—had been crouching at his door the past three years. And with the beastie skulking there, Jerry dared not cross any threshold; he dared not leave his home.

He never knew from where the troll had come or what had brought it or how it had gotten into his

185

home. Although Jerry called it a troll, he never truly knew it by name. He never saw it clearly either, straight on, anyway; he only caught glimpses of the thing out of the corner of his eye—a dark form, grotesque and twisted, creeping about in the shadows.

But whether it came from heaven or hell, whether it traveled there on foot or on an unearthly wind, whether it followed Jerry through the door or slipped under it like a serpent, whether it was a troll or a beastie or a demon, none of that mattered. The only thing that mattered now was it called Jerry's home its own.

That and it liked to kill.

Not everyone who came to the door or crossed the threshold. Not indiscriminately. It was smarter than that. It chose its victims carefully, one at a time. Although not always, it usually waited for its favorite night—like tonight, when little Halloween ghosts and goblins lurked in the neighborhood and came knocking at the door. For even if seen its existence wouldn't be questioned on Halloween— just another scary costume or decoration or maybe nothing more than a trick of light and shadow on a night when imaginations ran wild.

So, as he had the past two years, Jerry hid in the back of the house. He turned off all the lights inside and outside his home, hoping to discourage anyone from coming to his door, hoping to thwart the same needless bloodshed of the past.

But somehow he knew at least one foolish kid would brave the dark shadows, venture onto the porch, and sing out with that horrid refrain, "Trick or Treat." And like the others, that poor soul would be lost forever, never heard from again.

Except by Jerry, that is. He would hear the poor soul again.

Because the troll always took its prey to a secret place somewhere in the house then tortured them over a course of days. Jerry knew not where and dared not look. But the screams pouring through the walls kept him awake day and night until finally the victims fell silent, succumbing to the ordeal.

After death, their spirits joined the others that haunted the place and jabbered incessantly inside Jerry's head, as if *he* were guilty of murder and not the troll.

Voices of the dead bombarded Jerry's thoughts now—hissing their accusations, threatening their reprisals.

Maybe he *was* guilty. Maybe the sheer lack of trying to stop the beastie made him culpable. Maybe the fact that his home served as the troll's killing field made him responsible.

But how could he stop a supernatural force, a killing machine?

Jerry prayed that this night would end uneventfully, that the lack of light and activity from within his home would discourage anyone from coming to his door.

But his prayers went unanswered.

"Trick or Treat," a boy's familiar voice called from outside Jerry's darkened door, "Trick or Treat."

Jerry's breath caught in his lungs. He held it there, imprisoned, as if afraid that letting it loose would set in motion horrible and unavoidable events.

"Call again, Brian," a man's voice instructed. "I know he's in there. Your Uncle Jerry hasn't left the house in almost three years."

Jerry's held breath burst from within him. He scrambled to his feet. He thought he had recognized the boy's voice, but the man's voice confirmed it; his brother and nephew stood right outside the door, unaware of the danger crouching there.

"Trick or Treat," Brian called again.

Jerry stumbled to the kitchen table. He peered through the doorway and into the living room. From there, with his vision somewhat adjusted to the dark, he could make out the front door looming just ahead.

"Mike...Brian," Jerry called, "go away...get away from the door."

"Jerry, open the door," Mike called back, "let us in."

"Trick or Treat, Uncle Jerry," Brian chimed.

From the corner of his eye, Jerry caught a glimpse of the troll's twisted shadow. It darted toward the door, stalking its prey at the threshold, carrying in its grasp what looked like a large knife.

Jerry lunged toward the doorway between kitchen and living room but dared not go through it. Instead, he gripped the doorframe, digging his fingers into the wood until they bled, and shouted, "Go away...run...quick, get away...before it's too late."

If Mike responded, Jerry didn't hear. The voices of the dead now deafened him to all other sound. His world suddenly spun out of control, rocking him back on his heels. He stumbled about in the dark kitchen, unable to think. The mind-numbing voices in his head quickly turned to screams pleading for mercy.

And all he could do was join in with screams of his own.

◆◆◆

Jerry woke lying facedown on the cool linoleum of his kitchen floor. Moaning, he pushed himself up into a sitting position and cleared the cobwebs from his brain with the shake of his head. In a maddening rush, it came back to him—Mike and Brian at the door, the troll, the screams.

He scrambled to his feet, switched on the kitchen light, and staggered out into the living room. Within the eerie backlight from the kitchen, the opened doorway gaped at him as if in a mocking laugh. He longed to close it but dared not approach the threshold for fear the troll still crouched there in the shadows.

Jerry's brother and nephew were nowhere in sight. He could only guess as to their fate.

Then a thought came to him. Tiptoeing to the nearest wall, he put an ear to the hard surface and listened. A muffled groan greeted him from somewhere on the other side.

"Mike?" Jerry whispered. "Brian?"

Another muffled groan answered.

As he thought, they were somewhere within or behind the walls, just like all the others. The troll had taken them to its secret place, to its torture chamber.

Jerry had never been able to find it. But, then, he had never truly looked. Fear had always shackled him into inaction. Even the pleading screams from the troll's victims hadn't pushed him into rescue

189

mode. Instead, those beseeching cries for mercy had fallen on deaf ears. To drown them out, Jerry had played loud music through headphones.

That's why the spirits haunted him, cursed him, whispered vengeful nothings in his ear; he had never even tried to save them.

But they were mostly people he had never met, strangers he had never invited to his home. This was different. This was his brother, his nephew. He couldn't turn a deaf ear to them. He had to save them no matter what.

With his ear still pressed to the wall, Jerry followed the faint groan around the room until it led him back inside the kitchen and toward the refrigerator. He scrunched himself against the side of the appliance and listened intently. But before he could be sure of what he heard, the refrigerator turned on, clunking and humming, drowning out all other sound.

He stood back, scrutinizing the large appliance as if it were an alien machine beamed down to his kitchen from an orbiting starship. He listened to its incessant hum and startled when the refrigerator suddenly turned itself off and fell silent. He trembled even more when he heard the faint sound of groans and whimpers come from it, as if Mike and Brian were somehow held captive within its frosty walls.

But he knew that couldn't be.

Inspecting the refrigerator, he noticed the cord went to an electrical outlet a few feet away. Slowly, he moved toward the appliance and pulled the heavy thing away from the wall and out into the room.

Afterward, he stood back and stared at a closed

door, dumbfounded.

Why hadn't he put the refrigerator in front of the outlet to hide both it and the cord? Why would he put the large appliance in front of a door, hiding the existence of another room or maybe a basement?

Then he remembered. The refrigerator had come with the house. It stood where it always had, since the day he moved in. He never thought to move it. He was never told about the hidden door and whatever waited beyond it.

Studying the mysterious door, he contemplated its meaning.

He had always assumed that maybe the troll had followed him home, that it was somehow attached to him. But now, after finding this hidden door, he thought that maybe the beastie had come with the house, undisclosed by both the realtor and the former homeowner.

With that thought, a shiver slithered along Jerry's spine, and a skullcap of fear gripped his scalp. Surely he had found the troll's secret room, the torture chamber. Surely, he had found his brother and nephew.

He listened intently. Groans and whimpers came from the other side of the door. Although muffled, he heard them clearly enough.

He tiptoed toward the closed door. He had no workable plan, no idea how to proceed. He only knew he had to find Mike and Brian. And to do that, he knew he had no choice but to cross the threshold into the troll's lair.

His right hand held the doorknob in a death grip, squeezing it with white-knuckled intensity. But he couldn't bring himself to turn the knob.

What if he came face to face with the troll? What would he do?

It didn't matter. He'd think of something. He had to save Mike and Brian, no matter what. But he also needed to be smart about his rescue attempt. If not then they would all surely die.

Maybe he needed a weapon.

He released the doorknob and went to a kitchen drawer. From within it, he took the biggest and sharpest knife he could find, some kind of butcher's knife. He held the knife at the ready with his right hand. With his left hand, he turned the doorknob. As he slowly opened the door, it creaked like the rusty hinges of a vampire's coffin in an old horror movie. A long staircase greeted him on the other side. From where he stood, the stairs descended into what looked like a black hole. A stench ascended out of that blackness and slapped him across the face. A groan like that of a graveyard ghost rattled his nerves.

What little courage he had summoned now faltered. His trembling hand almost dropped the knife. He longed to slam the door shut and forget he had ever found the hidden basement. But if he did that then he sealed both Mike's and Brian's demise. He would have to live with their tortured screams for days. Afterward, their vengeful whisperings would join the others, haunting him until only his own death finally silenced them.

He couldn't live with that. He had to find a way to brave the basement.

From the corner of his eye, Jerry saw a light switch on the wall. He knew the light would give him away if the troll was indeed down there. But the

192

mere thought of venturing down the stairs and into that black hole made his stomach roil. Right now, just standing at the top of the stairs and looking down into solid darkness brought what felt like hot lava up into the back of his throat.

He could get a flashlight; he had one somewhere. But he held little hope that a narrow beam of light would settle his stomach and steel his nerves.

Without further debate, for better or for worse, Jerry switched on the light. The basement immediately brightened, but what he saw made him feel no better about descending those stairs than had the foreboding blackness.

Bloody clots of human tissue and hair clung to each step. Smears of blood stained them. Bloody hand prints streaked the wall and ran along the railing too—the troll's victims apparently putting up a futile battle to remain topside.

"My God," Jerry whispered.

Swallowing down an eruption of hot lava, he somehow forced himself to take that first step into perdition. With that first step came a second then a third, until finally he found himself just three steps from the bottom. From there, he peered about, searching for the grotesque and twisted form that had haunted his home for three long years. Thankfully, the troll was nowhere in sight, and the ghostly groans had fallen silent, as well.

But what Jerry saw and smelled appalled and sickened him more than anything he had experienced so far.

One big, square room stretched out before him, its walls covered in blood, hair, and human tissue like macabre wallpaper. Hand tools—both mechanical and electrical—littered a workbench and the blood-soaked floor. A stench of feces and death punched him in the gut and sent him reeling. The room looked and smelled like the workshop of a maniacal handyman.

As his gaze darted from one horrid sight to another, Jerry glimpsed two stainless-steel surgeon tables at the center of the room. Strapped to one was his brother's stripped body.

A coroner's Y-shaped incision split Mike open. Internal organs spilled out of him, across the table, and onto the floor, as if he had exploded from the inside out like overcooked macaroni and cheese in a microwave.

Jerry hunched over, vomiting onto his shoes. Even when nothing remained, he convulsed with dry heaves. Finally, he straightened and used his shirtsleeve to wipe slick remnants from his chin. To steady himself, he had to grab onto the soiled handrail as he stumbled down the three remaining steps. Averting his eyes, he staggered past Mike's desecrated remains to the second table.

There, Brian lay strapped and confined. The boy remained clothed and relatively untouched except for a large bump on his forehead, scrapes and scratches on his face and hands.

First Jerry felt for a pulse. It felt weak but steady. Then he tried to wake Brian by tapping the boy's cheek.

"Brian," Jerry whispered, "wake up…it's Uncle Jerry."

He unbuckled the belt from across Brian's chest and used the butcher's knife to cut the leather straps

194

away from the boy's wrists and ankles.

Tapping Brian's face again, Jerry whispered, "Brian, wake up."

The boy groaned. His eyelids fluttered.

"Come on, Brian," Jerry urged, "I'm going to get you out of here."

Groaning again, Brian opened his eyes. But the sight of Jerry with the butcher's knife must've been too much for the boy; his eyes quickly rolled back into his head, and he again lost consciousness.

Jerry let out a long, hitched sigh, realizing he should have put the knife down and out of sight. His traumatized nephew apparently couldn't tell the difference between uncle and troll, couldn't comprehend the difference between being harmed and being rescued.

"Okay," Jerry whispered, "I guess I'll have to carry you out of here."

He set the knife on the stainless-steel table and picked Brian up, cradling the boy in his arms like a baby. But Brian was no baby. He was a fairly sturdy nine-year old, getting heavier by the second.

Again, Jerry averted his eyes away from his dead brother as he hurried with the boy to the stairs. He rushed up the staircase, hardly believing his luck for not coming face to face with the troll. At the top of the stairs, he kicked the door closed with his foot and stood there in the middle of the kitchen, breathing hard, and barely cradling the boy in his aching arms.

What now? He had invaded the troll's turf and stolen its prey. It wouldn't be happy. It surely would come for them, soon, and he had stupidly left the knife downstairs in the troll's domain.

195

What he had to do was get Brian out of the house. But that was easier said than done. Jerry hadn't left this house in three years. How could he now?

Besides, the troll probably waited by the threshold, hidden just outside, waiting.

Jerry was convinced that was why he hadn't seen the beastie downstairs; it was playing with him, taunting him, daring him to take Brian and attempt an escape.

He carried Brian into the living room and set the boy on the sofa. The front door still stood open, mocking him. The unknown outside terrorized his soul and the mere thought of leaving his house after so many years gave him the shakes.

But then he thought of the troll and the misery of the last three years inside the house. What waited outside couldn't be worse than that, could it?

Jerry took a deep breath and gazed down into the innocent face of his nephew. That calmed him or at least resigned him to his fate. Whether he liked it or not, he had to get Brian out.

But the troll surely waited at the threshold.

What Jerry needed was a diversion, a way to get through the doorway and outside to safety without the troll noticing or caring, something big enough and bold enough to not only throw the beastie into turmoil but also destroy it at the same time.

Jerry hurried back into the kitchen, retrieving matches and a bottle of cooking sherry. Back in the living room, he threw the bottle at the wall nearest the drapes—glass shattering, flammable liquid splattering.

If this doesn't silence the voices then nothing

will, he thought.

"This is for Mike…and for all the rest," Jerry whispered.

Without further hesitation, he lit a match and sent it flying toward the sherry-soaked drapes. They ignited instantly, flames dancing up toward the ceiling and down toward the carpet. Within seconds, the fire grew from infancy into a roaring monster. With that monster came a choking, black smoke.

Now was his chance. He turned to scoop Brian up into his arms, but the boy was suddenly conscious and on the move, running through a maze of flames, crying out in terror.

"Brian, wait," Jerry called, "the troll…the threshold."

But the boy paid no heed to Jerry's warning. Instead, Brian kept moving through the flames, disappearing into the black smoke.

Jerry plunged into the dense blackness after the boy, heat scorching his skin, smoke stabbing his eyes and filling his lungs. Blindly, he reached out for his nephew but grabbed only flames. He screamed in pain and barreled his way toward the door. Tripping, he went down hard, knees hitting first, the rest of him following with a thud. He lay across the threshold, head and arms outside, the sweet scent of fresh air pushing the smoke from his lungs in long, violent coughs, the rest of him still captured within the fire-ravaged house, hot flames licking at his legs and feet.

Brian sat on the porch, back against the railing, coughing, gagging, rubbing his eyes.

"Brian, help me," Jerry called. He reached for his nephew, fingers barely touching the toes of the boy's sneakers.

Brian dropped his hands and stared at Jerry with wide-eyed terror. He screamed, kicking free of his uncle's outreached hands and jumping to his feet.

"Brian, help me," Jerry pleaded. He struggled to crawl the few feet to freedom, but he couldn't move, as if something inside the house had a hold of his legs. "Help me, Brian," he pleaded again, reaching out to the boy.

Brian moved sideways along the railing, feeling his way to the stairs, eyes riveted on his uncle.

"Brian, the troll's got me," Jerry screamed. "Don't leave me."

At the top of the stairs, Brian turned and ran, Jerry's screams giving chase. The boy made it down the stairs and across the lawn to the safety of the sidewalk. He turned back just in time to see the house collapse, crashing down into a blazing pile of rubble and finally silencing his uncle's tortured shrieks. Burying his face in his hands, the boy sobbed and wailed.

In the distance, fire engines and police cruisers joined the boy's lament, their mournful songs resounding through the Halloween night.

◆◆◆

Brian sat up in bed, unable to sleep. Outside, a storm brewed. The wind whistled through the eaves and shook the trees. The limbs of the tree right outside his bedroom periodically banged against the rain gutter—wood against metal. A flash of lightning ripped open the black sky, and far off thunder rumbled like a waking monster in the night.

Pulling the covers up to his chin, the boy scanned the dark room through tear-soaked eyes. It

198

was Thanksgiving, but he had nothing to be thankful for. Yeah, he had survived the Halloween ordeal. But both his dad and his uncle were dead. His mom cried constantly and hovered over him every second. Policemen still visited, asking him questions he didn't know how to answer. Doctors asked him questions too, insisting he share his feelings.

What he felt was scared, all the time now. During the day he jumped at every sound, every trick of light and shadow. Sleepless nights were spent huddled under the covers, just like this night, hiding from the thing that stalked him.

It was there now, in his bedroom. He couldn't see it, but he could feel its presence in the pit of his stomach, like when he ate too much candy. He shivered and pulled the covers tighter to ward off the weird feeling of spiders creeping along his arms and scurrying across his scalp. He found it hard to breathe, like when that bully at the playground pushed him down and sat on his chest. And the pleading screams of his uncle haunted his thoughts.

Tree limbs banged against the rain gutter. The patter of rain struck the windowpane. A flash of lightning lit up the bedroom for a split second, revealing a grotesque and twisted shadow lurking near the door; Brian caught a glimpse of it from the corner of his eye. He screamed simultaneously with a boom of thunder.

"Brian," his mom called, her footsteps pounding in the hallway, coming fast.

A rhythmic rain now thrashed against the window. The tree limbs kept time on the metallic gutter like a bass drum.

Lightning flashed across the room again.

In that second, Brian again glimpsed the twisted form. It crouched at the threshold of his room, large knife in hand.

But darkness soon swallowed it whole.

"Brian, are you all right?" his mom asked, opening the door.

"Mom, don't come in," Brian hollered.

But thunder buried the warning under a deafening boom.

Lightning flashed again, revealing his mom framed in the doorway, about to cross the threshold, the twisted form ready to strike.

But darkness quickly followed.

And thunder buried the screams.

Christmas-Time Gremlins
A Sequel

Revenge.

That's what the three gremlins wanted. It was as pure and simple as that.

Revenge.

Under the cover of night, the gremlins plowed through the snow-encrusted forest of the North Pole. The trek had them breathing hard, icy vapors escaping from their mouths. They stopped at the tree line just outside Santa's village. Frost and snow clung to them, and despite the knotted, tangled hair they sprouted from head to toe, the little beasts shivered and huddled together for warmth. Three sets of beady, red eyes darted to and fro, taking in the layout of the compound:

A huge lighted Christmas tree stood at the center, a Christmas star shining brightly atop it. Circling the tree were Santa and Mrs. Claus' log cabin, the mammoth Toy Factory, the Post Office that received thousands of letters a day from boys and girls around the world, the reindeer barn where Dasher, Dancer, Prancer, Vixen, Comet, Cupid, Donner, Blitzen, Rudolph, and their families lived, two dormitories for the single, adult elves—one for the men and one for the women, the Tracking and Weather Station equipped with a satellite dish on its roof and radar so the movements of Santa's sleigh on Christmas Eve could be followed and weather conditions around the world could be monitored, and the Tech Center where the latest in technological advances were discovered and implemented in the hopes of making Santa's job easier. Smaller domiciles dotted the landscape between the bigger buildings, serving as private homes for the married elves and their families.

The Post Office, the Tracking and Weather Station, and the Toy Factory were dark and showed no signs of life. The reindeer were bedded down for the night, and the barn too was devoid of light or movement. Lights, however, brightened the windows of the Claus' log cabin, the dormitories, and most of the private homes. Fireplace smoke rose out of every chimney. Lights shone through the windows of the Tech Center, as well—someone apparently burning the midnight oil. The grounds themselves, though, were empty—no one evidently willing to venture out into the frigid, late-night air.

The three gremlins crouched at the forest's edge. Hatred for Santa filled their black hearts. For in their tiny, demented minds, they believed that Santa had murdered one of their own. And for no reason either. The poor gremlin Santa had killed was just doing what gremlins naturally do—eat human flesh. To save a boy named Chuck and his family, Santa had smacked their fellow gremlin upside the head with a shovel, cracking its skull wide open, bone fragments, tissue, and blood spraying all about.

The gremlins couldn't stand by and just let that go. They had to exact revenge; Santa had to pay…and dearly.

But how?

That was the question they were unsure how to answer.

Yes, the gremlins had dagger-like teeth and massive pointy claws, more than effective weapons for ripping and rending flesh.

But Santa was much bigger and heavier; whereas gremlins only stood no more than four feet tall.

And yes, there were three of them and only one of him.

But the big man's bothersome elves were always about, lurking nearby, watching out.

Besides all that, the gremlins at heart were cowards. And they knew it. They wanted their revenge—their pound of flesh—but none of them—even together—had the courage to face their sworn enemy head on. They were by nature creatures that chose smaller, defenseless prey to victimize and to feed upon.

That's why they hesitated, even after having traveled so far for retribution, even as vengeance burned at the suppurating sores in which they called their hearts.

"What to do?" a gremlin hissed, frosty breath visible in the night air.

Shivering, they crouched and huddled together, each looking at the other for an answer.

"Kill Santa," another gremlin hissed back.

"Yes, but how?" the third gremlin muttered.

They had come all that way with no plan of

attack, and their miniscule brains couldn't come up with one now.

But then chance or divine luck stepped forth, for the door to Santa's log cabin opened. Out stepped a large man. The man didn't wear Santa's red suit of legend and song but rather a heavy parka—hood pulled up over his head—gray snow pants, and black boots. Still, the largeness of the man and the fluttering, long white beard indicated that he must be Santa. Besides, he had come out of the cabin the gremlins knew to be Santa's home. Even dimwitted creatures such as these could figure out the man's identity based on those clues.

"Follow," a gremlin hissed.

The other two nodded and hissed in agreement.

Snow crunched underfoot as Santa crossed the compound, strolled past the lighted Christmas tree, and continued on toward Tech Central.

The three gremlins slowly trailed the old man with stealth and cunning to his destination. They snuck through the door Santa had carelessly left open. Once inside Tech Central, they shook snow from their hairy bodies like dogs coming in from the rain. Then, they crept to the shadows in a far off corner.

There, they lurked, waited, bided their time, and listened.

◆◆◆

Santa stomped his feet. Clinging snow broke free of his boots. Flipping the hood of his parka back and off his head, he crossed the main room of Tech Central—basically a warehouse crammed full of large dedicated servers, network servers, desktop computers, laptops, video recorders and monitors,

MP3 players, televisions, DVD players, and countless other electronic gadgets. The room was also equipped with a laboratory that boasted multiple Bunsen burners and a labyrinth of tubing that ran to test tubes and beakers too numerous to count, all full of various bubbling and smoking concoctions of different colors and densities. Colorful lights flashed and blinked all around. Hums, static, crackles, beeps, and other odd noises resounded throughout the room. In fact, the entire place had the look and the sound of a modern-day mad scientist's secret lair.

An elf waited for Santa in front of a bizarre contraption that looked to be a cross between a large computer server and an Indy race car.

"Gideon," Santa called as he approached, "this better be worth getting me out of my warm house this time of night." The usually jolly, old man came to a screeching halt. He looked non-too jolly as he gawked at the machine, dumbstruck. "What have you done to the Time Control Machine? Gideon, you better not have broken it."

Gideon whirled toward Santa. He showed no fear of Santa's surly mood. In fact, his face beamed with pride, and he grinned from ear to ear. "I didn't break anything, Santa. I improved it."

Santa groaned. "Not again," he muttered. He took a second look at what used to be a beautiful machine. He said, "It looks like something a robot barfed up."

"Humph," Gideon said. "You've never liked change," he chided.

Santa looked properly chagrined. "You just better not have broken it that's all," he murmured.

205

Gideon sighed. "Don't worry. The machine still controls time, slows it down, so you can deliver presents around the world in one night."

"It better," Santa said," otherwise there'll be a lot of disappointed children."

"But now we can not only control time," Gideon said, puffing up his small chest, "but we can also travel through time…and space too."

"Huh?" Santa looked perplexed.

Gideon held out his arms as if presenting the contraption for the first time. "Ta-da," he said, "it truly is a time machine now. We can send you into the future or back into the past. And not only can you transcend time, but you can transcend space too."

"Time travel isn't possible," said Santa, "and even if it was, *you* surely wouldn't be smart enough to pull it off."

Gideon folded arms across his chest and scowled. "If I'm smart enough to figure out how to slow time then why ain't I smart enough to figure out how to travel through time? Answer that!"

Santa shrugged. "Okay, explain it to me."

Gideon unfolded his arms and grinned. "The Earth is considered two dimensional because every point on Earth's surface can be specified by two coordinates—longitude and latitude," the elf explained. "But the universe is four dimensional, so locating an event in the universe and traveling through what I call spacetime requires four coordinates. I not only need to know where to go—longitude and latitude—but also how high to go and when to arrive. Four coordinates—four dimensions."

Santa rolled his eyes. "Gideon, I just—"

"Think of the Earth not as a sphere," Gideon interrupted Santa's interruption, "but as a helix—a long piece of spaghetti spiraling around the Sun's world line through time. The distance in time for the helix to complete a turn is one year, and this helix is Earth's world line, its path through spacetime. That's four-dimensional thinking," he said proudly. "All real objects have four dimensions," he continued, "width, breadth, height, and duration. Your four dimensions for example appear to be approximately six feet tall, maybe one to three feet thick, two to three feet wide, and over four hundred years in duration. You, like the Earth, have a world line. Yours starts with your birth, snakes through space and forward in time, threading through all the events of your life, and ends of course at your death. In theory, as a time traveler, your world line could somehow loop back in time, where it could even intersect. In other words, an older version of you could meet up with a younger version of you, and the two of you could shake hands. The younger version would then continue his life, becoming old and eventually loop back to that same event where the two versions again meet." Gideon took a deep breath. "Whoa, this time traveling stuff gives me a headache sometimes."

Santa rubbed at his large belly and muttered, "Gives me a belly ache." He dared to pause before demanding, "Now, enough with the quantum mechanics—"

"I think you mean physics," Gideon pointed out.

Santa snapped, "Quantum mechanics...physics...whatever. Get to the point.

207

Just tell me why we need the machine and how it works."

"Well," Gideon ventured, "we could use it to fix past mistakes."

Santa tapped his foot and gave the elf a stern look. "What mistakes?"

"Y-You know, those very few times when a nice kid got accidentally put on the naughty list...and vice versa. We could give a toy that wasn't given but should've been...and...take away a toy that was given...but shouldn't have been."

Santa cleared his throat. "I don't remember any such mistakes ever—"

"Anyway," Gideon cut Santa off, rushing forward, wishing he could go back in time and choose his last words more carefully, "most scientists agree that time travel to the past would be possible if you could go faster than the speed of light. Unfortunately, light speed is the universe's ultimate speed. So I used Einstein's theory of gravity that he called 'general relativity' to solve the problem."

Santa continued to tap his foot and roll his eyes. "Get to it, Gideon."

"Einstein's theory states that under certain conditions spacetime can curve in ways that permits shortcuts through it," Gideon explained. "Basically, visualize time as vertical, space as horizontal, and your world line as a straight line, up and down, always going towards the future. Bend spacetime into a cylinder and your vertical world line bends with it, returning to where it started by circling the cylinder; your world line would complete what is called a *closed timeline curve* even though it seems as if you're always traveling forward into the future."

Gideon paused before continuing, "It's like when Magellan and his crew left Europe traveling steadily west and eventually sailed completely around Earth to return to Europe, where the voyage began. That wouldn't have been possible if the world was flat. Well, this machine bends spacetime, making it cylindrical, which makes it possible to revisit an event in your past even though you're still traveling forward in time."

Gideon took a deep breath.

"Gideon," Santa said as calmly as he could muster, "you still haven't told me how the machine works—the mechanics."

"Oh," Gideon said.

He leaned forward into the machine. Unlike a car, the mutated mechanism had no wheels. But Gideon had installed a seat for the time traveler, a dashboard, and a steering wheel, all just like a car's, onto the once perfectly rectangular machine. On the dashboard were dials and controls.

"You set these controls to your four coordinates," he said. "Let's say you want to go back to the time when your mother left you on the doorstep of the Kringles."

"Let's say, I don't," Santa complained.

But Gideon ignored his boss' reservations. "We set longitude, latitude," he continued as he turned the controls, "height, and time." He stopped fiddling and stepped back. "There, those coordinates should allow you to revisit that time and that place."

Santa shuffled from foot to foot. "Maybe I don't want to. Did you ever think of that?"

Gideon looked aghast. "You always said that you wished you could meet your real mother. And what about the man who saved you from the same terrible creatures that killed your mother. He gave that belt buckle you cherish so much to your adoptive father Karl Kringle, so he in turn could give it to you? Wouldn't you like to meet that mysterious man?"

Santa unzipped his parka and stared down at his golden belt buckle with the large, raised initials SC engraved into it.

"That man and that belt buckle are the reasons you chose to use the name Santa Claus rather than Kris Kringle—the name your adoptive parents gave you." Gideon paused. "That man's your namesake," he continued.

Santa shook his head. "But wouldn't I run the risk of altering the timeline? I think it's called a...*paradox*. Couldn't I somehow change things...maybe for the worse...just by being there?"

Gideon thought for a moment. Then, he said, "A physicist named Igor Novikov advocates what he calls the *principle of self-consistency*."

Santa's raised his bushy eyebrows. "What's that mean?"

"It means if you witness a previous event, it must play out just as before," Gideon explained. "Time travelers can visit the past, but they can't change it."

Santa nodded. "An appealing notion," he admitted.

He kept staring at the belt buckle. The idea of going back in time and meeting not only his real mother but also this special man who according to the Kringles saved him as a baby from a horrible death was like an itch he couldn't scratch.

Finally, he asked, "If I go, how do I get back?"

Gideon grinned. "I'll show you how to reset the coordinates to bring you back to this exact time and place. It'll be like you never left."

Santa zipped up his parka. "Okay," he said, with only a slight hesitation, "let's do it."

Gideon grinned. "All aboard the Gideon Express to the past," he proclaimed.

Santa climbed behind the wheel and settled into the seat.

"Hey, you know…you're going to meet yourself too," Gideon said, "as a baby. Cool beans."

Santa didn't think it "cool beans." Second thoughts and serious doubts were already swirling about in his head. And somehow, all of those misgivings upstairs traveled downstairs to his large belly, resulting in flip flops and cartwheels. Besides that, his heart thumped and sweat glistened on his face.

"Better do this," Santa croaked, throat dry, "before I back out."

"See this lever?" Gideon asked. He pointed to what looked like a stick shift. "And see the four displays on the dashboard that are all set to zeros?"

"Yeah," Santa answered.

"Just push the lever slowly forward until the four displays match the four, preset coordinates on the other displays above."

Santa nodded. He took a deep, hitched breath. He said, "Wish me luck."

Gideon stepped back, far out of the way. "Luck," the elf said with a wave of his small hand.

211

Swallowing hard, Santa slowly pushed the stick forward.

The engine began to softly hum. Colored lights on the dashboard flickered and blinked. The machine trembled. The zeros on each display began to move forward.

Santa pushed on the stick more.

The changing numbers picked up speed. The lights blinked faster too. The hum grew into a high-pitched shrill. The time machine no longer just shook but now rocked back and forth like an out of control washing machine.

"Whoa!" Santa cried.

The world around him began to fade, becoming transparent, as if dematerializing. His head spun. The high pitched shrill and the thud of the machine as it rocked and hopped against the hard floor became almost deafening. And the machine's agitation didn't do his late-night dinner any good either, for partially digested spaghetti and meatballs spun in his belly, and spicy sauce sped up his esophagus, burning the back of his throat.

"Gideon," Santa screamed, bits of his upchucked dinner spewing from his open mouth.

Even though hundreds of tiny black spots attacked his already blurred vision, Santa still somehow saw the three horrible demons rush out of the shadows, their hideous screeches resounding over all other noise.

"No!" Santa cried.

◆◆◆

The three gremlins crouched and huddled in a dark corner. All around them were strange sights, sounds, and smells. In fact, they saw Santa and the elf standing in front of an odd-looking contraption, the likes they'd never seen before.

"What to do?" one gremlin hissed.

"Shhh...listen," another whispered.

The third gremlin nodded in agreement.

So the three gremlins leaned forward, straining to hear Santa and the elf's conversation over the other noises in the room. The elf was waving his arms and pointing at the odd machine while explaining something. He used a lot of big words and fancy phrases the gremlins couldn't possibly hope to understand—their miniscule brains incapable of such comprehension. But they did hear something that made them sit up, take notice, and concentrate; they did understand enough of what the elf said to know that Santa was going on a trip to the past. They couldn't grasp how or why. But that wasn't necessary. What they did understand was that the odd machine would miraculously take Santa back to a time when he was a baby.

"Santa...baby," a gremlin hissed, looking at his two cohorts.

"Baby easy to kill," another gremlin said. "Santa baby die in past...Santa no more...now."

Hunched in the shadows, the three demons chuckled with evil glee at that sudden and startling insight.

"We go to past," the other gremlin whispered. "Kill baby. Kill Santa. Easy."

"Eat baby Santa too," the first gremlin quietly declared. "Roasted baby meat delicious," it added.

All three gremlins licked their lips with thick, black tongues.

While the gremlins hatched their wicked plan,

Santa climbed aboard the time machine. The elf instructed Santa on how to use it, and before the gremlins knew it the soft hum of an engine started and colored lights flickered and blinked and the odd machine trembled. Soon, the lights blinked faster and the engine's hum grew into a high-pitched shrill and the machine rocked and bounced as if it was either going to explode or shoot off into space like a rocket. Then, Santa yelled.

That's when the gremlins noticed that they could see right through Santa and the machine as if both man and contraption were nothing but ghosts.

"Hurry," a gremlin shrieked, "before too late."

As one, all three of the gremlins rushed out of the shadows, charging across the room, screeching like terrible beasts.

"No," Santa cried.

But it was too late. The gremlins had made it past the elf, launched themselves through the air, and latched onto the time machine just as it disappeared.

◆◆◆

Gideon's machine successfully transcended time and space but didn't just quietly appear in the year 1555, on a deserted street in Amsterdam—a small fishing village in the Netherlands that had been settled on the river Amstel. Instead, it burst upon the scene and fell from the sky like Dorothy's house in the *Wizard of Oz*.

First it was just Santa and the gremlins' screams and screeches that shattered the still night air. Then there was a loud thud as machine hit snow-encrusted ground. Chunks of metal and electronic components broke apart on impact, ejecting like shrapnel from

214

an exploding bomb. Santa and the three gremlins were thrown into the air right alongside the wreckage.

Santa's large frame hit the ground the hardest, rolling end over end in the snow until finally coming to a stop facedown.

The three gremlins were luckier; all three landed in a huge snowdrift on the side of the street.

Santa groaned. He pushed himself up, wiping snow from his face with a gloved hand and spitting the white stuff from his mouth. With a grunt, he turned himself around and sat in the snow, taking stock. Luckily, the streets weren't paved in this time period which made the landing, if not completely painless, at least more bearable. The snow helped break his fall, as well.

Unluckily, a chunk of sharp metal had pierced his right side, just above his belt. It had gone right through his thick parka, sunk deep into his flesh, and now stuck out of him like a large, metal splinter. Blood soaked into the parka around the wound and dripped to the ground, staining the white snow a deep red.

Santa reached around, grabbed the chunk of metal, and pulled with all his might. A sharp wail escaped his lips as the metal splinter slowly tore free of flesh and clothing. Packing snow into the wound to stop the bleeding, Santa scanned the area.

Fortunately, the hour was late and no one had been out and about to witness the strange commotion. However, all the noise had begun to raise suspicion, for lights now brightened some windows in the surrounding homes.

Santa spotted the Kringles' toy shop about a

block away. Lights winked on in the upstairs windows, above the shop, where his adoptive parents lived. At the front door stood a startled woman cloaked in shadow and light. At her feet was a basket. In the basket, swathed in blankets, was a crying baby. As the three gremlins charged across the snowy road right for her, the woman screamed.

The gremlins, though, made no sound at all as they pounced on their prey. The poor woman fell without much struggle. Her scream silenced quickly as pointed claws and sharp teeth ripped into flesh. Now snarling and growling, the beasts fought each other as they ate with ravenous hunger.

Horrified, Santa screamed, "Mom!"

He struggled to get to his feet, but the pain in his side and the slippery snow sent him back to the ground. Growling like a wild animal at the sight of his birth mom being torn to pieces and eaten, Santa again pushed up and this time managed to climb to his feet. He swayed on unsteady legs, clutching at the bleeding wound in his side.

"Stop," he roared.

But the gremlins had already finished with his mom and were advancing toward the baby.

Holding his side, Santa ran as fast he could through the snow, toward his childhood home and the terrible creatures that had just murdered his mother.

The gremlins hurried to the baby. One of them yanked the baby from his basket and blankets, clutching the small boy in one hairy hand, a pointed claw at the ready to rip and rend.

"Stop," Santa roared again.

The gremlin did. All three beasts turned toward

216

the sound of Santa's cry. They squealed at the sight of the large man rushing toward them.

Then there was the sound of windows being pushed open.

"What's going on out there," a man yelled from the safety of his home.

"What are those things?" hollered another.

"No time," the gremlin holding the baby hissed. "Take. Kill later."

With their prize in hand, all three gremlins turned and ran, making good their escape just as the door to the toy shop flew open.

Karl Kringle stopped just outside the doorway. First he stared in horror at the dead woman at his feet. Then he looked up to see three horrible-looking creatures running off into the night. Even more horrifying was the sound of a crying baby. A pitiful sounding plea for the creatures to stop rose above the baby's cries, and then an old man ran past the toy shop and down the street, in hot pursuit of the monstrous kidnappers. The man ran with a hitch and held his side as if injured but kept on going. The next thing Karl Kringle noticed was the trail of blood the old man left behind in the snow.

Santa saw his adoptive father framed in the doorway of the toy shop. But there was no time to stop, no time to explain. His very existence depended on catching the gremlins before they could kill and eat the baby. If that happened, he would be no more…or rather he would never have been at all. The ramifications of that event happening was not only personally frightening but also earth shattering for all the girls and boys around the world throughout future time.

So on Santa struggled, holding his side, trailing the gremlins' footprints in the snow. And before he knew it he was through town and out into the countryside. He plowed through heavy snowdrifts for a mile or two before coming to a dense forest. There, he stopped for a brief moment, trying to catch his racing breath and to rest his tired legs. Taking his hand away from his side, he inspected the blood-soaked glove. With a grunt, he bent over, grabbed some snow, and packed the frozen stuff into the wound.

He was losing blood fast. And the gremlins would soon stop to eat their prize. He knew he had very little time.

He almost laughed at that thought.

"I should've stayed in my own time where I belonged," Santa muttered.

Without anymore hesitation, he crossed the tree line and plunged headlong into the forest. Following the three sets of gremlin tracks through the snow-covered countryside had been easy; they hadn't even tried to cover their trail. But within the forest, the trail had gone cold. Not as much snow had made it past the treetops to the ground below. Besides that, it was darker and harder to see. The few footprints there were seemed almost impossible to follow.

Santa stopped in frustration. He breathed hard. His heart thumped. His side throbbed. Blood soaked his gloved hand, his parka, and even his pants, running down his leg into his boot. Panic swelled in his chest like a sharp pain. Everything around him looked the same; it seemed he'd been traveling in circles. What was he going to do?

To calm himself, he thought about a time

paradox:

He still had time. The baby had to still be alive. Otherwise, he himself would no longer exist.

Santa groaned. The pain in his side proved he still existed.

But where had the gremlins gone?

Santa sniffed the air.

"Smoke," he muttered.

He sniffed the air again. It was faint, but the air definitely smelled of smoke. Then a sudden realization hit him like a sucker punch.

"They're going to roast me!"

Now he sniffed the air with more purpose. He followed the smell of the campfire to a small clearing. There, he stopped behind a large tree, spying on the scene before him.

One gremlin worked at the campfire, hunched over it, adding wood and stoking the flames. Another gremlin gathered more wood at the other end of the clearing. Clutching the baby by his foot and dangling the child upside down, the third gremlin watched over the other two as if supervising the whole affair.

The baby didn't move or make a sound. Not for the first time, Santa worried that he was too late. But then he reminded himself of the paradox:

The baby had to still be alive. Otherwise, he himself would no longer exist.

Santa pulled his bloody hand away from his side; he was bleeding to death, and he knew it. There was no time to waste. No time to really develop a plan. He had to act now or die.

Howling like a crazed werewolf, Santa bolted into the clearing. He rushed the gremlin holding the

219

baby.

The gremlin let loose a surprised squeak. It dropped the baby as it backpedaled away from the charging big man.

The baby hit the ground hard, but Santa had no time to worry or react to the possibility of the child being hurt. He only had time to grab the retreating gremlin by the throat. Lifting the beast into the air, he throttled it senseless, hearing the life choke out of it as the other two demons attacked. One landed on Santa's back, its dagger-like teeth sinking into his neck. The other landed on his chest, its claws ripping across his face.

Santa flung the dead gremlin aside. Spinning like a top, he managed to dislodge the gremlin on his chest.

That gremlin flew across the clearing. It hit a nearby tree trunk, its head cracking open like a ripe melon. Chunks of skull, brain matter, and blood sprayed the clearing as the gremlin fell to the ground with a heavy thud.

The gremlin on Santa's back held on for dear life. Its claws dug deeper into the big man's flesh. Its teeth were still embedded in his neck.

Santa stopped spinning. With purposeful precision, he fell backwards onto the fire, pinning the gremlin within the flames. A shrill yowl shattered his eardrum as flames sputtered around both him and the burning gremlin.

When he felt the gremlin's teeth leave his neck and its claws release their grip, Santa rolled away and kept on rolling until he had put out the flames on himself.

The gremlin remained in the fire, no longer

yowling, no longer moving. A strong odor of singed hair and burnt flesh permeated the night air.

Lying on his back, Santa coughed and gagged on the stench. His breathing sounded labored; fluid seemed to fill his lungs rather than air. Blood poured from the wound on his side, soaking the ground.

But a baby's cry put a smile on his face; the boy was alive.

Then Santa heard footsteps nearby. But he couldn't seem to move. It felt as though something very heavy sat on his chest and pinned him to the ground. All he could do was gaze up at the night sky and the stars that twinkled above the treetops as he listened to the footsteps move away from him, seemingly toward the crying baby. Before too long the footsteps were on the move again and the baby's cry was getting louder, closer. Seconds later, Karl Kringle knelt down, and Santa stared up into his adoptive father's kind, gentle face.

"I'm sorry I couldn't get here sooner," Karl Kringle said, his voice cracking. Tears welled in the man's eyes. "I'm very sorry."

Santa smiled. "It's alright," he croaked. "Baby's safe?"

Now Karl Kringle smiled. He held the baby up for Santa to see. "He's fine. You saved him."

Santa coughed up blood. "The baby's yours now," he croaked.

"I'll raise him as my own," Karl Kringle promised. He put a gentle hand on Santa's chest. "Now save your strength," he added.

"Not much time," Santa whispered. "Unzip my coat."

Karl Kringle did as requested.

Santa coughed again, hacking up more blood. When finished, he asked, "See the belt buckle?"

Karl Kringle nodded.

"Take it," Santa said, coughing. "When he's old enough, give it to the child and tell him about me."

"I will," Karl Kringle promised. He ran a finger along the raised initials SC that were stamped into the golden belt buckle. "Who are you?" he asked. "What name should I give the boy when he asks?"

"Santa Claus," the dying man said with his last breath.

♦♦♦

Gideon left Tech Central just seconds after Santa and the gremlins disappeared into spacetime. He locked up tight and headed home to his wife and children, secure in the knowledge that Santa would wake tomorrow morning in his own bed and in his own time, safe and sound.

Many years ago, when Santa had told the story of him being left on the Kringle's doorstep, his mother being killed by monstrous, little beasts, those same beasts kidnapping him, and then him being saved by a mysterious man who gave Karl Kringle the belt buckle and called himself Santa Claus, Gideon somehow instinctively knew that Santa himself was that same mysterious man. That's when the elf began his quest to make a machine that could transcend time and space because he also somehow knew that he himself had a very important role to play in helping Santa fulfill that destiny.

Gideon stopped outside his door. He rubbed at his forehead.

Paradoxes in time actually did give him terrible headaches when he really thought about them. Even so, he couldn't seem to stop himself from reanalyzing this one.

In point of fact, unless Santa went back in time and saved the baby him from the gremlins—which hopped aboard and also went back in time—then there'd be no Santa Claus.

Oh, his mother would've still left him as a baby on the doorstep of the Kringle's toy shop; Kris Kringle as a person would've still existed, being brought up by the toy maker and his wife.

But that Kris Kringle's world line would've taken a totally different path through time. Without his world line looping back in time to intersect with itself, Kris Kringle would've never become Santa Claus.

No Santa...no presents for all the children throughout the world on Christmas Eve. It was as simple as that.

Gideon thought harder, still reanalyzing the paradox over and over again in his mind.

Maybe he should've told Santa the whole truth, though, before he embarked on his journey through spacetime.

With that thought plaguing his mind, Gideon turned and looked at Santa's log cabin, suddenly worried.

He had only told Santa half the truth about the *principle of self-consistency* when he said that time travelers can visit the past, but they can't change it. What the elf purposely neglected to explain was that according to the theory time travelers don't change the past because *they* were always a part of it. In other words, time travelers don't alter the past but rather fulfill it.

223

At the time, he was sure that Santa would've never understood. He was sure it was better that Santa never know.

Gideon sighed.

Now—in the quiet of the night, with just his worrisome thoughts for company—he wasn't so sure.

Holiday Madness

Fred Wiehe teaches Creative Writing and Academic Writing to both children and adults. He is a member of the Horror Writers Association. His biography has been included in the 2005 edition of *Who's Who in America* and the 2006 edition of *Who's Who in the World.* Besides *Holiday Madness*, he is the author of four more books:

His supernatural thriller *Strange Days* was called, "a creepy, hair-raising, chill bumping read" and "a winner in its genre" by *Midwest Book Review. Baryon Magazine* said, "Wiehe has written a solid adventure with a metaphysical twist!" Jonathan Maberry—2007 Bram Stoker Award-winning author of *Ghost Road Blues*—said, "Strange Days by Fred Wiehe is one of those wonderfully strange, mind-twisting stories that never goes where you expect it to go, and always delivers shocks and thrills. This puppy begs for film or graphic novel adaptation." Nicholas Grabowsky—author of *Halloween IV* and *The Everborn*—said, "[Strange Days is] a novel of ageless evil told with wicked abandon and stylish prose." Weston Ochse—2006 Bram Stoker Award-winning author of *Scarecrow Gods*—said, "Wiehe's punchy prose pounds us with dementia, mis-adventure and enough multi-dimensional mayhem to KO Quinten Tarantino and leave him smiling as he hits the floor."

Other novels written by Fred Wiehe include the sci-fi thriller *Starkville*, the horror-suspense novel *Night Songs*, and the dark-fantasy novel *The Burning.*

Mr. Wiehe has also just finished his first screenplay titled *Freak House*, which has been optioned by Elftwin Films in LA.

Visit Fred Wiehe online to find out more. Go to www.fredwiehe.com or www.myspace.com/horrorauthor or www.facebook.com/fred.wiehe.

By Nicholas Grabowsky:

"Nicholas, I salute you!" ---Clive Barker

BLACK BED
SHEET

LaVergne, TN USA
09 November 2010
204170LV00001B/40/P